# There she was.

He could see Paige through the window. She was talking on the phone as she worked at the counter. As she hung up, she met his gaze through the glass. She flashed him a smile and his heart stopped between beats.

Paige McKaslin shone like a morning star, like the gentle light that remained even when all other stars had gone out. She yanked open the door. "You're a lifesaver, Evan."

That troublesome tightness was back in his chest. He padded through the kitchen door. Once he was far enough away from her, the ability to breathe returned, but the emotion remained jammed in his throat. The impact of her smile was still powerful and his heart pounded crazily.

Never had he reacted to a woman like this. As he took his seat at the counter, he wondered if he'd hit his head harder than he'd thought.

**Books by Jillian Hart**

Love Inspired

*The McKaslin Clan

## *JILLIAN HART*

makes her home in Washington State, where she has lived most of her life. When Jillian is not hard at work on her next story, she loves to read, go to lunch with her friends and spend quiet evenings with her family.

# A HANDFUL OF HEAVEN

## JILLIAN HART

Steeple Hill®

Published by Steeple Hill Books™

STEEPLE HILL BOOKS

Steeple
Hill®

ISBN 0-373-87349-2

A HANDFUL OF HEAVEN

Copyright © 2006 by Jill Strickler

www.SteepleHill.com

**Printed in U.S.A.**

When I am afraid, I will trust in You.
—*Psalms* 56:3

# Chapter One

"Hey, Mom!" The diner's back door slammed shut with an icy gust of wind. Heavy boots tromped across the clean kitchen floor. "I took the garbage out. The bathrooms are spotless. I even cleaned the milkshake machine."

Paige McKaslin turned from the prep table to take one look at her seventeen-year-old son who was giving her "The Eye," as she called it, the one meant to charm her. He'd been using it effectively since he was fifteen months old. Alex was tall, blond and athletic and rangy. One day he would fill out those wide shoulders of his, but in the meantime he was eating as though he had two hollow legs. "You just had supper. Do you need two chocolate doughnuts?"

"You don't wanna stunt my growth, Ma!" He pretended to be shocked but those baby blues of his were twinkling. "Can I go? The movie starts at eight and Beth doesn't like to miss the previews."

One thing a mother didn't want her teenage boy to have—aside from the keys to her car—was a girlfriend. Especially a girl who did not belong to their church or any church in the county. "You behave, and remember what I told you."

"Yeah, I know, I'll be a gentleman. As if!" He rolled his eyes, his grin widening because he'd achieved victory. "I'm outta here."

"Drive safely. It's icy out there."

"Yeah, yeah. I know. I passed my driver's test, remember?"

As if she could forget. Letting go was hard but necessary. She bit her lip. Alex was a good driver even if he was young and inexperienced. "Don't forget to call me at the diner the second you get home— before your curfew."

"Mom, I know the drill. See ya!" He pounded out of sight, whistling. The back door slammed shut and he was gone.

Off to any kind of danger.

Paige bussed the eight plates from the Corey family's party.

She'd thought nothing could be more worrying than having a toddler. Alex had been such an active little tyke, and fast. She'd been a wreck trying to stay one step ahead of him, worrying what he would try to choke on next. Or electrocute himself with next. Or fall off of and break open his skull next. How she'd worried!

Little had she imagined all those years ago that her sweet little boy was going to turn into a teenager and do something even more dangerous than try to stick pennies in electrical sockets. He would drive. She dealt with that the way she always dealt with anxiety—she just tried hard not to think about it.

"I had that same look of sheer panic," Evan Thornton commented as she shot down the aisle. "It was right after each of my boys got their licenses. I don't think I've calmed down yet, and they're both in college now."

"No, of course you're not calm because they are probably out there driving around somewhere."

Evan chuckled, and the fine laugh lines at the corners of his eyes crinkled handsomely. "Exactly. It's hard not to be overprotective. You get sort of fond of 'em."

She heard what he didn't say. There was no stronger love than a parent's love. "Lord knows why." She balanced the plate-filled dishpan on her hip. "Would you like a refill on your fries?"

"If it's not too much trouble."

"Are you kidding? I'll be right back. Looks like you need more cola, too." She flashed him a smile on her way by.

Evan had been frequenting the diner most evenings. Bless her regular customers who gave this tough job its saving grace. She did like making a difference, even if it was only cooking or serving a meal that they weren't in the mood to fix for themselves.

On the way down the aisle, she stopped to leave the bill with a couple who looked as if they had wandered in off the interstate. They still had that road-weary look to them. "Is there anything else I can get you?"

"Oh, no thanks." The woman, who was about Paige's age, tried to manage a weak smile, but failed. Sadness lingered in her dark eyes. "I suppose we ought to be heading on."

"Will you be traveling far? I have a friend who owns a nice little bed and breakfast in Bozeman. It's the most restful place and reasonably priced. If you're staying in the area, I could give her a call for you. No pressure, I just thought I'd try to help." Paige slipped their bill on the edge of the table.

"Sounds like just what I need, but we have a funeral we're expected at in Fargo in the morning. The airlines were full, and so we're driving straight through." Tears rushed to the surface.

Paige whipped a pack of tissues from her apron pocket and slipped it onto the table. "I'm so sorry."

"Th-thank you." The woman covered her face, her grief overtaking her.

Her husband shrugged his shoulders. "We're going through a tough time."

"I know how that is. Let me know if you need anything."

Not wanting to intrude, Paige backed away, the memory of her own losses made fresh by the woman's grief. The day her parents had died had been the day after her sixteenth birthday, and it was as if the sun had gone out.

Time had healed the wound, but nothing had ever been the same again. She was thirty-eight, on the edge of turning thirty-nine—eek! But time had a strange elasticity to it, snapping her back over two decades to that pivotal loss.

*Maybe there's something I can do to make the woman's journey easier.* In the relative calm of the late evening diner, Paige bustled into the back, where the evening shift cook was sitting at the prep table bent over the day's newspaper.

Dave looked up, his expression guilty. "I thought I got everything done I needed to. But here you come looking like I'm in trouble. What'd I forget to do?"

"Nothing that I've found. I can come up with something if you'd like."

"Are you kidding? I just got set down. It was a heavy Friday rush. I'm about done. I've been standing in front of that grill for twenty years and every night just seems longer."

Sometimes Paige forgot how much time had passed, not only for Dave but for her, as well. She'd been in this place for so long that the decades had begun to blur. She still saw Dave as the restless wanderer just back from Vietnam. He'd come in for an early-Saturday lunch and stayed on as one of the best short-order cooks they'd ever had.

In a blink, she saw not the past but the present, and the man with liberal shocks of gray tinting his long ponytail, looking the worse for wear. "Go on, get home. And don't forget to take some of the leftover cinnamon rolls with you. They'll be a nice treat for breakfast tomorrow."

"I wasn't complainin', you know. I don't mind stayin' in case you get a late rush."

"I'll handle it. Now go, before I take hold of the back of your chair and drag you out of here." Paige turned to snag one of the cardboard to-go boxes. A few quick folds and she had two of them assembled and ready.

"Well, if you insist." Dave's chair grated against the tile floor as he stood.

"I do." She split apart a half dozen of the last rack of cinnamon rolls—why they hadn't moved this morning was beyond her. Yesterday the whole six dozen she'd been regularly buying had disappeared before the breakfast rush was over. She popped the sticky iced treats into the waiting boxes and added a few of the frosted cookies, too—those hadn't moved, either—then snapped the lids shut.

"Here. Go. Hurry, before a bunch of teenagers break down the door and take over the back booth." She slid one box on the table in his direction.

"Only if you promise to call me if you get slammed."

"Deal. Now beat it." She pounded through the doorway and into the dining room where the grieving woman and her husband were just gathering up their things to leave.

It took only a few moments to fill two extra large take-out cups with steaming coffee, stick them in a cardboard cup holder, and fill a small paper bag with sweetener, creamer and napkins.

"That sure hit the spot." The husband slid the meal ticket and a twenty on the counter by the till. "That was the best beef stew I've had in some time."

"My Irish grandmother's family recipe. I'm glad you liked it." She rang in the sale with one hand while she pushed the baker's box and cup holders in their direction. "Here's a little something to keep you alert while you're on the road. It's a long stretch between rest stops once you're past Bozeman. I'll be praying for a safe journey."

She counted back change, but the husband held up his hand, shaking his head. "Keep the change. That's mighty kind of you."

"Bless you." The woman teared up again and headed for the door, wrapping her overcoat more tightly around her.

After taking the box and cup holder, the husband joined his wife in the entryway and held the door for her. They stepped outside, the door swished closed, and they were gone.

"That was awful nice of you."

Paige startled, spinning around to see Evan Thornton watching her along the length of the serving counter. "I don't know about nice. I had extra cinnamon rolls that I didn't want to go to waste."

"Still. Not everyone would go to the trouble."

"Lord knows times like that are tough enough. We've all been there, battling heartbreak."

"Yes, we have." Evan's face hardened, and he turned away, staring at his plate.

He's known heartache, too, she remembered. She didn't know the details, but he'd been divorced long ago. She knew just how much pain that could give a person.

Maybe it was just her mood today, but the shadows seemed to darken quickly. Maybe a storm was on the way.

Night fell like a curtain until she could see the lighted reflection of the diner in the long row of front windows and her own tall, lanky form standing there, nearly as dark as the world outside.

She saw something else in that reflection. Evan Thornton turned on the bar chair in her direction. Her stomach gave a funny tingle. Was he watching her? And why on earth would he do that? When she looked his way, he wasn't studying her at all but recapping the ketchup bottle, his attention squarely focused on the task.

Funny. Maybe it was her imagination. Or maybe he'd been drifting off in his own thoughts, the way she'd been.

The back door clicked shut and the screen door banged, telling her that Dave had fled while the getting was good. It might be Friday night, but she expected it to be a quiet one from here on out. There were no games or matches at the high school. The middle school's spring musical pageant had been last week, and weekend nights were typically quiet in the lull after Easter. It didn't help that winter had decided to sneak in for a final showdown and the hailstorm earlier would keep most folks at home and off the slick streets.

Except for her son, wherever he was. She checked the wall clock above the register. Enough time had passed that he should be off the roads and safely inside the movie theater. She wouldn't have to worry about him again for two more hours when the movie was over and he'd be out on the roads again.

That left her to worry instead about the growing

list of things needing to be done. Like the extra cleaning she'd been trying to fit into the quieter times, and the general ledger, which was still a mess on the desk, and the paperwork for the ad she needed to place in the paper—

She was back in the kitchen before she realized she'd made a conscious decision to go there, apparently lured by the exciting thought of cleaning behind the refrigerator, which was the first thing on her list that needed doing.

Now, if she could only find the energy, she'd be in seventh heaven. What she wanted was chocolate. Lots of cool, soothing, rich chocolate.

"Hey, Paige?" It was Evan Thornton calling from the front.

Trouble. She knew the sound of it well enough. There was no disguising the low note of concern in his rumbling baritone. Now what?

Four steps took her into the narrow hallway between the kitchen and the front. The thought of taking a chocolate break and then cleaning behind the refrigerator vanished at the sight of water creeping from the men's bathroom. Not just a trickle, but a shining sheet of water silently rushing from wall to wall and nosing like a giant amoeba toward the front counter.

There Evan was, a formidable shape of a man on the other side of the creeping waterway. "I could engineer a bridge for you."

She blinked. Was it her imagination or was he practically smiling? She'd never known Evan Thornton, an engineer, to have a sense of humor. Then again, she really didn't know him, which was the way she liked it and wanted to keep it. Getting too close to men, especially single, handsome, and apparently nice men, always led to trouble. At least, in her experience. "Uh, no, I'll risk the current without a bridge, thank you."

Why was it that some men looked better with a little distinguished gray in their hair? He shrugged those gorgeous shoulders of his, strong and straight. "Just thought I'd help. Let me know if you need me to toss you a lifejacket. Or a buoy. Or a marine? No?"

She blinked again. There he went again, and this time he was definitely almost smiling. The gentle upward curve of his hard mouth cut the hint of dimples into his lean sun-browned cheeks. She felt a flutter of interest down deep in her heart, and dismissed it. She was a woman after all, sworn to a single celibate life, but that didn't mean she was dead. "Call for help if I don't return."

"You can't deal with that yourself."

"Watch me." She swept past him, wading through the torrent streaming down the hallway. What would it be like to be free of this place? She'd been here so long, she couldn't even imagine it. But she would sure like to.

She was planning to put the diner up for sale this summer. She'd been accepted at the nearby university to begin classes in the fall.

"Do you want me to call a plumber?" He spoke with that polished baritone that could make a girl take a second look.

She absolutely refused to turn around. She didn't need a second look. She wasn't interested in Evan or in any man. "Not yet, it might be something I know how to fix."

"Are you telling me you're a good cook and a handyman, too?"

"Just because I'm a woman doesn't mean I can't use tools."

*Right.* Evan watched Paige McKaslin march away from him, all business. She was a study in contradiction. On the surface, she was brusque, crisp and coolly efficient. A man might draw the conclusion that she was made of ice.

But if he watched close enough, he'd see a different woman. A woman who was vulnerable and over-worked and tender. He'd seen the look on her lovely face when the crying customer had said they were on their way to a funeral. She cared. And she hadn't charged the couple for the hot coffee and snacks to help them along on their all-night drive.

She wasn't as coolly tough as she let on, either. Not judging by the way her straight shoulders had slumped when she'd first eyed the leak cascading down the hallway. She was handling the flood now, marching up the water-filled hallway braced like a warrior facing battle. She was a small woman, and that came as a surprise. She was always moving, a busy, no-nonsense, get-things-done woman. Now, as he watched her, he realized just how lovely she was.

Why he was noticing, he couldn't rightly say. He'd given up on women and the notion of trusting them ever since he'd come home to find a quick note from his wife taped to the refrigerator door explaining why she was leaving him. That wasn't all. She'd drained their bank accounts, maxed out the credit cards with cash advances. She'd even liquidated their nest egg of stocks and bonds.

All very good reasons never to notice another woman again.

So, why was he standing here watching as Paige disappeared into the men's restroom? Water lapped around the toes of his shoes. A smart man would go back to his seat and finish off the rest of his meal and contemplate the dessert menu. He would not be staring down the hallway, feeling as if he ought to lend a hand.

Why? That made no sense. He wasn't much of a handyman, so there was very little he could do to help, unless it was to turn off a valve. Paige had been clear she could handle the leak and any required tools. She was a competent woman; he'd have to believe her. Maybe the reason had more to do with her beauty than her competence.

No, that didn't make any sense. After Liz had broken his heart, wrecked their family, and destroyed his financial security, no woman's beauty could affect him. No, the reason he was standing here as the flood rushed past him into the dining room had nothing to do with Paige McKaslin. Not one thing. His chest constricted with a pain worse than a root canal.

He thought of his absolutely quiet, very empty house and took a step upstream. Water sloshed over the top of his shoes and wet his socks. Helping her was the only decent thing to do. It wasn't likely that she could find a plumber this time of night. And certainly not fast enough to save her entire diner from water damage. At the very least, Paige would have a serious repair bill on her hands.

He'd see if he couldn't help keep that to a minimum, he thought, as he knocked on the closed men's bathroom door and shouldered it open. Water resisted, and when he shoved harder, he saw why. What might have started as a small leak had resulted in complete erosion of the major water pipe to the sinks. Water gushed out of the floor full-force now, and Paige sat beside it, her face in her hands, her shoulders slumped.

In utter defeat.

Evan's heart twisted. He stepped forward, blown away by an overwhelming need to help her. To make this right.

# Chapter Two

This is going to wipe out the diner's monthly profit. And a lot more as well.

Paige scrubbed at her face. Tired, she was just so tired. She had to call a plumber. She couldn't do this herself—this was no minor repair. Already the water level had risen a few inches. And since the break in the pipe was below the shut-off for the sinks, the main line would have to be shut off.

Not only that, but the clean-up was going to take time—*hours* of hard work. Don't think about that, she commanded herself as she climbed to her feet. One step at a time. First she had to get this water turned off.

"Where's the main shut-off valve?" A man's voice came out of nowhere, bouncing off the bare walls.

She jumped, splashing the water around her. "Evan. I didn't know that you were there. What are you doing? You're going to ruin your shoes."

"I've had worse problems. This is an older building. Don't tell me the shut-off is underneath."

"There's a crawl space, but you can't go down there." She waded across the room, splashing and slipping, as fast as she could go.

Evan had already turned and was wading down the hall. "Evan!"

He was gone with a splash, but like the ripples ringing outward from his movements in the water, the effect of his kind presence remained.

You're only imagining that the kindness in his voice is personal, she told herself as she slogged after him. Waves washed against the tile protection along the walls and threatened to start wetting the wallboard at any time.

Evan had gone back to his seat, right? As she scurried down the hall she caught a glimpse of the nearly empty dining room. Evan wasn't in it.

Men. This was why she didn't have one. You couldn't trust them to do what you said—you couldn't trust them at all, not as far as you could throw them. She grabbed her coat from the kitchen closet and the flashlight from the top shelf.

The chill in the wind cut through her, tearing at the edges of her coat, and she zipped it up tightly as she ran. The light from the windows gave just enough light to thin the shadows as she tripped along the icy flagstone path around the far edge of the building.

The trap door was flung wide open and the scant light down below gave her no hint of what was happening. Had Evan already found the valve and turned it off?

He peered up at her from the shadows below. Dust streaked the top of his head. "You wouldn't happen to have any tools on you, would you?"

Those dimples had dug into his cheeks again and caught her off guard.

"I—" Her brain shut down. Tools. He was talking about tools. "You don't need one for the shut-off. Just let me—"

"I found the valve, but it's stuck open."

"It's stuck? No, it can't be. The handle has to be jiggled just right. It's temperamental." She barreled down the wooden steps, swiping cobwebs out of her hair. "Let me try it."

"Do you have a toolbox upstairs?"

"There's a kit in the kitchen closet by the door but—" She stumbled along the uneven ground and went down on her knees by the valve. He was already gone. It didn't matter. She wrapped both hands around the small metal handle and pulled. Nothing.

She strained harder. Nothing.

Okay, what she needed was a little more muscle. She braced her feet, used her weight as leverage and heaved with all her strength. The pipe groaned. The valve screeched a millimeter and then stuck as if it had been cemented into place.

No, this can't be happening. She took a step back and her heel splashed in something wet. Water. It was coming through the floorboards at the end near the bathrooms. What was it doing upstairs?

Before panic could set in, Evan was back, thundering down the steps and into the narrow space, stooping as he went, the toolbox clinking with his movements. He dropped the box at her feet and snapped it open. Her hand shot out for the wrench but he'd already stolen it.

"Hey, this is my job," she decided loudly.

He didn't seem to care, as he was already shouldering next to her and fitting the wrench into place. "It's just rusted some. Let's hope this doesn't break the pipe."

"And if it does?"

"There's always the shut-off at the meter in the street, but let's—" he paused as he put some muscle into his effort "—hope that it doesn't—come—to that."

Metal screeched in protest.

"Is it working?"

"Not yet. Could you aim the flashlight right here? It'd help if I could see what I'm doing."

"Sure." She moved close to point the beam at the stubborn valve in the narrow corner. "I keep imagining that I'm going to need an ark to rescue the last of the customers I left in the dining room."

He gave the wrench a little more muscle and the screech of old copper pipes told him he was making some difference. "If it comes to that, I'll engineer you one."

"Then I'll be even more in your debt." The gentle curve of her mouth eased into a ghost of a smile as she leaned closer to give the flashlight she held a better angle.

She smelled of cinnamon and roses. Cinnamon from the kitchen, he guessed. And roses from her lotion. The subtle aroma made him take notice. His chest throbbed. Heartburn, he thought, dismissing it as he felt the valve give a tiny bit. At his age, chest pain wasn't a good sign. Being forty-two was a thrill a minute.

He was no longer young, but he wasn't anywhere close to being old. Just in between. Which is pretty much where he'd been all his life anyway. Wasn't that what Liz had always mourned? He wasn't a stand-out kind of guy. Just average. Average looking, average earning…just average *everything*.

And that hadn't bothered him much over the years until this moment.

The wrench froze in place, and as he moved into a better position, he bonked the top of his head hard on a thick wooden beam. Stars lit the dimness before his eyes a split second before pain reverberated through his skull.

Great going, Thornton.

"Are you all right?" Genuine emotion softened her lean face, and in the spare glow of the flashlight's dim bulb, he saw concern fill her eyes.

"I'm fine. I've got a hard head."

He couldn't help noticing how lovely she was. Her heart-shaped face was classically cut with a delicate chin, a straight nose and wide, startlingly blue eyes. Dark feathery bangs spilled over her forehead, making him want to smooth those silky wisps away from her eyes. A band tightened around his chest like a vise.

That's it, I'm cutting down on French fries.

He gave the wrench a little more torque, gritted his teeth and pushed for all he was worth. The stubborn wrench didn't move a millimeter and then slowly, with a high-pitched squeal, it began to give. The pipes groaned. Evan groaned. His arms burned as he clenched his jaw and gave it everything he had.

The valve closed.

"Oh, Evan! You did it! Oh, I never could have done that by myself. You are incredible! Thank you so much!"

"It was nothing." He removed the wrench and realized he was shivering.

"Nothing? You've only earned my eternal gratitude. It's freezing down here. Come on up and we'll get you something hot to drink." She grabbed the wrench from him, and her warm, satin fingers brushed his.

Suddenly he totally forgot about being half frozen. He noticed the faint blanket of freckles across her nose. Her skin was flawless, her cheekbones high and chiseled, her mouth full and her chin delicate.

The vise around his chest clamped so tight he felt close to suffocating. He shouldn't be noticing how beautiful Paige McKaslin was, because in the end it didn't matter. He'd sworn off women, and that especially included noticing the beautiful ones.

He cleared his throat. "No, I'm fine. And as for your eternal gratitude, why don't we call it even? You've served me plenty of good meals over the years."

"Yes, and you've paid for them."

"But I didn't have to cook 'em for myself. See?"

"That's not the same." She headed up the stairs.

He did his best to behave like a gentleman and not notice how trim she looked in her worn jeans or the delicate cut of her ankle showing above her sneakers. He hit the light switch and climbed up after her in the dark. Something cold and icy pecked against his face.

"It's snowing." She towered over him, the tool-box in one hand and the flashlight in the other, aiming the shaft of light down the ladder, growing slippery with icy snow.

"Great. That will mix nicely with the dust and cobwebs." The icy flakes slanted through the flashlight's golden beam and pelted him as he landed with his feet on solid ground. "You're going to need a plumber."

"Very observant of you." She knelt to grab the heavy trap door.

He beat her to it. "Go in where it's warm and call Phil's Plumbing. It's in the phonebook. He's my brother-in-law. You tell him I said to get over here pronto and give you a good price while he's at it."

"Thanks, Evan." She marched away, blending with the dark until she was gone.

He didn't know if it was the icy storm or the dark that made him feel keenly alone. Well, he was used to being alone these days, he thought as he hefted the heavy door into place.

There used to be a time when he'd been so busy, making a living, running after the boys, looking after laundry and meals and bills that he ran on constant exhaustion. It was painful to remember, and yet it only felt like a few days ago when he'd dropped into bed well after eleven each night and bemoaned having not a second to call his own.

Funny, how he missed that now. How he'd give just about anything to go back in time. Those days had whipped by so fast, he'd forgotten to hold onto the good in them. And now...well, his sons were grown up and both doing well. Cal was in college and Blake in law school. Grown men, or at least grown-up enough that they didn't need him like they used to.

As he made his way around the building to the back door, satisfaction settled over him like the snow. It was good to do something useful. To make a difference. There was no way Paige could have handled that valve on her own, but she certainly hadn't been squeamish about crawling into a narrow dank space.

There she was. He could see her through the window in the back door. She was talking on a cordless phone tucked between her chin and shoulder as she worked at the counter. She met his gaze through the glass. She flashed him a smile, a rare one of the sort he'd never seen from her.

His heart stopped between beats. The usually cool and collected Paige McKaslin shone like a morning star, like the gentle light that remained even when all others stars had gone out. She yanked open the door. "You're a lifesaver, Evan."

That troublesome tightness was back in his chest. He managed a shrug, but he didn't manage to breathe. "I take it you got a hold of Phil."

"He's on his way." She headed straight to the counter. He couldn't help being struck by the long pleasant line her arms made as she hung up the phone. She had beautiful hands, slender and graceful.

And exactly why was he noticing this? Dumbstruck, he padded away through the other kitchen door, the swinging one that led to the far end of the dining room, so he could avoid the pool of water.

Once he was far enough away, his ability to breathe returned, but the emotion remained jammed in his throat. At the doorway, he glanced over his shoulder at her. She was working her way around the corner and didn't seem to notice him looking.

He took one shaky step into the dining area and along the empty aisles. Only one other couple remained in the diner, finishing up their steak dinners. He fumbled onto the stool and leaned his elbows heavily on the counter. The impact of her smile remained, and his heart pounded crazily in his chest as if he needed a defibrillator.

Never had he reacted to a woman like that. Not even to Liz when he'd first fallen in love with her. What was happening? He didn't know. But as he took his seat and grabbed the last of his fries, his taste buds paled. Everything seemed suddenly dim and distant. It was a strange reaction. Maybe he'd hit his head harder than he'd thought.

His pastor, his friends, his sons and even his brother-in-law, whom he'd kept in contact with after the divorce, all told him he ought to start dating again. That he should find some nice woman to share his golden years with.

*I don't want to admit to being anywhere close to having golden years.*

"Evan?

The fork clamored to the plate. His fingers had somehow slipped. When he managed to meet Paige's gaze, he made sure he didn't notice that she was a beautiful, graceful woman with a tender heart. He forced himself to see the efficient businesswoman, who had taken his orders, served his meals and counted back his change over the years. *That* was the only Paige McKaslin he could allow himself to see.

"Department of Health rules. I can't be open for business unless I have working restrooms." She set a big paper bag on the counter between them and a take-out cup, capped, next to it. "Your extra order of fries, a slice of banana cream pie, I know how you like it, and a hot cup of that gourmet decaf you some-times order."

"Uh…thanks." What he needed was to head straight home, empty house or not, and put some distance between his stirred-up emotions and Paige McKaslin. What he needed to do was to sit in the quiet of his home, the same house where his wife had cheated on him and finally left, and then he'd remember why being alone was the right choice.

"Here." She reached beneath the counter and began dropping packets into the bag. "Let me make sure you've got napkins and a few things. Is there anything else I can do for you?"

"The pie would be fine. How much do I owe you?"

"Nothing, goodness. After your help tonight, this is on me. Please, you didn't even get to finish eating."

"No, forget it. I pay my way." He pulled out his wallet and she held up her hand.

*Men.* Paige appreciated Evan's pride and his ethics, but she had some of her own. "If you insist on paying for this meal, then I'm only going to give you the next one free. In fact, maybe I'll do that anyway." She turned toward the mature couple ambling down the aisle. "You, too, Mr. and Mrs. Redmond. I see that twenty you left on the table."

"Well, dear, we're not freeloaders, and we were nearly done anyhow," Mr. Redmond kindly answered as he took a toothpick from the holder near the register. "You have a good night now. You still make the best steak in the state."

"My mother's secret spices." Paige made a mental note to give the Redmonds their next meal free. She had the best customers anyone could wish for—they were so understanding! She grabbed the small white sack containing the baker's box she'd filled in the kitchen and intercepted them at the front. "A little something for later."

Mr. Redmond was not opposed to the gift of dessert and held the door carefully for his beloved wife. They disappeared together into the storm.

Sweet. What must it be like to have a bond like that? Paige couldn't help the pang of regret or the pull of longing in her heart. She was thirty-eight years old, too old to believe in fairy tales, so why was she still wishing for one? The long painful years after her husband's departure and the following divorce had taken their toll, as had the years of shouldering responsibilities for her family. Working sixteen-hour days seven days a week had worn her to the bone.

What she needed was a vacation.

No, what she needed, she corrected herself, as she waded to the hall closet, was a time machine so she could go back twenty years, grab that naive eighteen-year-old she'd been by the shoulders, and make that foolish, stars-in-her-eyes girl see the truth about life. A truth that the grown woman in her had come to accept as a cold, hard fact.

There was no such thing as true love and no real knights in shining armor. Anything that looked like a fairy tale was either an illusion or simply wishful thinking.

Okay, that sounded bitter, but it really wasn't, she thought as she hauled out the mop. She sounded cold, but her heart wasn't that, either. If anything, Paige felt foolish. Think of all the time and heartache she could have saved herself had she understood that truth earlier in her life. Her road would have been so much smoother had she seen the world—and the man she'd married—for what was real instead of what she'd wished them both to be.

If she had, she could have focused on what truly mattered—and only on that. She could have avoided wasting energy on dreams that only faded, on hopes that true love would walk into her life one day.

The hope that she'd find a good man to love had faded over time, bit by bit, shade by shade until it was nothing at all.

That was how she'd been living for a long, long time. She swiped the mop through the water, thinking that she'd been happier this way. Alone was good. She was strong, capable and independent. She was also safe from all the harm a man could bring to a woman. Sad, trying not to remember the long-ago love she'd been unable to save, she wrung the mop, listening to the water tap into the plastic bucket like rain.

As she worked, she listened to the sounds of Evan gathering up the bag and ambling down the aisle. His steps were deliberate and slow, as if he were in no hurry to leave. He drew to a stop in the breezeway between the eating area and the front counter. "Do you want me to hang around until Phil gets here?"

"That's nice of you, but I'm used to being alone here after dark." She swiped the mop through the cold water and wrung the sponge head well. "I do appreciate your help tonight. Not everyone would have gotten up to help me."

"Glad I could make a difference. With my boys gone, I don't get to do that much anymore." He cleared his throat as if he had more to say, and could not.

What would it be like to come home to an empty house, she wondered? To open the door and know that her son would not be in his bedroom downstairs with his dog, listening to music or munching on potato chips or sacked-out fast asleep?

It had to be a long stretch of lonely, she thought as she went back to mopping. She didn't know what to say as Evan walked past to snag his jacket from the coat tree, she couldn't help noticing that he'd gotten pretty dirty crawling around under the diner. Dust streaked his slacks.

She bent to squeeze water from the mop head. "Uh, are those dry clean only?"

"No way. Don't even worry about it." He didn't look at her as he slid into his black jacket, pulled a baseball cap over his head and leaned against the door.

"Drive safe out there, Evan. The roads have to be a mess."

"You be safe, too." He cleared his throat, slid a ten and a five on the counter and took the sack. There was a challenging glint in his dark eyes as he ambled past, as if he were daring her to give the money back.

The bell overhead jangled as he strode into the night. "I'll see you tomorrow."

"Uh, yeah, that would be great. I'll be waitressing."

"Then I'll be ordering."

He stared at her for a beat, as the night began to engulf him. In the moment before the shadows claimed him completely, she saw the essence of him, not the physical, not the expected, but the steady strength of a good man.

The door swung shut, and she was alone. Snow pinged against the windows, driven by a cruel wind, and she swore she felt the echo of it deep in her heart, in a place that had been empty to romantic love since before her son was born.

And how foolish was that, that she was wishing for the impossible now? No, not exactly wishing, but thinking that it was possible again.

I'm more tired than I thought, she told herself with a chuckle as she turned the dead bolt and went back to her mopping.

# Chapter Three

The house was dark. He'd forgotten to leave a light on again. Evan fumbled along the kitchen entryway. Cal had gone off to school what? seven, eight months ago, and he still couldn't get used to him being gone. It hasn't been so bad when Blake had left, for he and Cal had made the adjustment together. But this…having them both gone, it felt like he'd walked into someone else's life.

But this was his life now. He was a free man, unencumbered and carefree. Shouldn't it feel better than this? Evan tossed the keys and his battered gym bag, and slid the sack from the diner onto the counter, pushed the door to the garage shut with his foot and listened to his footsteps thump through the lonely kitchen.

Let there be light. He hit the switch and a flood

of brightness shocked his eyes. He'd been outside so long, his eyes had gotten used to the darkness. The drive home had been slow and long and pitch-black. The headlights had been nearly useless in the rapid snowfall. And now, this place seemed too bright and too glaringly empty to feel like a home.

Well, he was just feeling lonely. It was Friday night, after all. Maybe one of the boys had had time to call in. That thought put some bounce in his stride as he left his briefcase on the kitchen table and leaned to check the message light on the phone recorder. Nothing.

Okay, young men had more fun things to do on Friday nights than to give their old dad a call. He was glad for them both. He wanted them to be out there, living their lives and doing well. It's just that he hadn't figured on how his own life would stand still when they were gone.

The flier one of his clients had sent him was sitting on the edge of the counter. He'd meant to toss it with the rest of yesterday's mail, but he hadn't gotten around to it yet. The apple-green paper seemed to glow neon in the half light and he pulled it out so he could look at it properly.

A Bible study for the rest of us. A bold carton caption stretched above a cartoon-like pen-and-ink drawing of a middle-aged man in his recliner. "The youth have their own lives, and the singles and the seniors have their activities. What about the rest of us? Come join us for Bible study, dessert and fellowship at Field of Beans."

That was the coffee shop in town—and Evan knew Paige's relatives owned it. That was a bonus, he suddenly realized. Plus, it was an evening meeting, something he could do after work. Something besides cleaning out the horse barn, that is.

He folded up the flyer and slid it in with the stack of bills needing to be paid. That was something he'd been meaning to do—study his Bible more. Now that he had the time. Maybe this was a solution to one of his lonely evenings. Maybe he would take everyone's advice—not to date but to get out and do the things he'd been putting off when he'd been so busy raising his sons.

The phone rang while he was on his way through the family room. One of the boys? Hope jolted through him. He snatched up the cordless receiver on the second ring. "Hello?"

"Is this Evan Thornton?"

"Uh…" In his excitement, he'd forgotten to check the caller ID screen. "Yeah. Who is this?"

"This is Michael from First National Bank, how are you this evening? I want to tell you about our new identity theft program—"

At least it wasn't bad news. "Not interested. Goodbye."

He hung up the phone, glanced around the room at the TV remote that was on the coffee table where it belonged and not flung and lost somewhere in the room, at the chairs pushed in at the table instead of all shoved around askew. There were no stacks of books or heaps of sports equipment and coats lying around, all needing to be put away.

Would he ever get used to the quiet, to the orderliness, to the emptiness? Standing alone in the family room, which had been put into tidy order by the cleaning lady, he felt at a loss. This didn't feel like home anymore.

As he headed upstairs to change out of his work clothes and into his barn clothes, he realized this was what it meant to be unencumbered and carefree, a free man again. There was no phone ringing off the hook, no kids traipsing through the house.

Just the telemarketers and him.

He'd always known his boys were a great blessing. He'd given thanks to the Lord every night as he'd lain down to sleep, but he'd never stopped to see the treasured gift that each day really was, and that, for all of those eighteen years, they were surprisingly fleeting.

"Well, that should just about do it." Phil the plumber tried to stomp the snow off his work boots. But considering the mud he'd picked up from the crawl space, it was a hopeless cause anyway. "I've double-checked the length of the pipes and couldn't find a drop anywhere. I think we've got the problem licked."

"Music to my ears. Thank you." Paige dropped the scrub brush into the soapy bucket, where she'd been cleaning the water line against the bathroom wall. "I appreciate this so much. I know it was a long drive out here, and it's going to be worse going back."

"Before you get all misty on me…" He gave a friendly—but not too friendly—wink. "I've got bad news. You're gonna have to replace some of this pipe. It's gonna be expensive, and if you want, I can work up an estimate. I can either do it for all new water lines, or I can do it in phases and we can just do the worst stuff first. You just let me know."

Bad news? Did he say bad news? No, he had that wrong; this was *devastating* news. The small allotment she put faithfully into the savings account every month for repairs would never be enough. She didn't have to go grab the latest bank statement to know that she couldn't afford to replumb the entire diner.

She also knew how lucky she'd been tonight. The damage could have been worse, and as it was, she could open for business as usual in the morning. She'd only lost three hours of business tonight. Not bad, considering. Heaven was gracious, as always, and she was thankful. "Why don't you work up the bit-by-bit estimate?"

"Fine by me. I'll send it with my bill."

Already dreading the amount due, she handed him a sack with the last of the cinnamon rolls. "A little something for your breakfast tomorrow. You drive safely out there now."

"I've got four-wheel drive." Phil hefted his big toolbox to the door and stopped to retrieve his parka. "I'll get the stuff in the mail on Monday. Thanks, ma'am."

When had she become a "ma'am"?

Probably about the same time her son had learned to drive. Thank God for hair color that covered the gray and intensive eye cream. Worry could do that to a girl. Stress was her middle name these days, and that combined with her age didn't help. She wasn't quite sure where all the time had gone—wait, erase that. She did. She'd spent probably seventy-five percent of the last twenty-two years right here in this diner.

After seeing Phil out and locking the door behind him, she glanced at the clock. The movie ought to be getting out about now. Great, she could get back to worrying about Alex being out there on these roads. Maybe what she needed to do was to expend some of that nervous energy and *clean*.

So she kept her eye on the clock as she scrubbed down the grill and wiped the counters, tables and chairs. Then she tackled the rest of the floor that hadn't been flooded, mopping until the tile squeaked beneath the mop head and her cell phone was ringing in her back pocket.

A quick glance at the caller ID window revealed her home number. Good. That meant Alex was home safe and sound—and even five minutes before his curfew. How great was that? "Hey there. How was the movie?"

"Good. You can stop worrying now. Notice the time? I'm calling you *before* eleven. What do you think about that?"

"It's unprecedented, and it makes me suspicious. Worry and suspicion are a mother's job."

"Yeah, yeah, I know. So, are you gonna be home soon?"

That question made her suspicious, too. "You didn't happen to notice a leak in the bathroom before you bugged out of here, did you?"

"Nope. I'd have told ya, even though Beth was waiting for me. Why? What'd I do?"

"Nothing. I had a leak in a pipe, that's all. Are you getting ready for bed, or are you going to get lost in your new video game?

"Uh, nope, I wasn't playing my X-Box, but thanks for reminding me, Ma." He sounded pleased with himself. "Just kidding. You want me to go out and feed the horse for you?"

He was volunteering to do barn work? There *had* to be something wrong. That wasn't normal teenage behavior. "Okay, what did you do?" Expecting the worst, Paige hefted the bucket toward the kitchen. "Don't tell me you dinged the truck."

"No way."

"Hit somebody on the way home?"

"Hey, I'm innocent. I'm just trying to help my poor tired mom."

Help? Now she was suspicious. She maneuvered the bucket up to the industrial sink and up-ended it. "Okay. Out with it, young man. What did you do? What are you trying to soften me up for?"

"Nothing. I just thought I'd be a good son for a change." There was a grin in his voice. "Don't worry."

"Yeah, I'm still suspicious, though."

"You go right ahead, Mom. You'll see." He sounded extraordinarily happy.

Could it be her son was moving past the surly teenager stage that even the best of kids went through? No, that was too much to hope for. "I'll see you when I get home. I'll be leaving in about ten minutes. Think you can have your teeth brushed and your prayers said by the time I get there?"

"Aye, aye, captain." With a chuckle he clicked off the phone.

Yep, something was definitely up with that boy. She snapped the cell shut, slipped it back into her pocket and rinsed the bucket. Done. Well, done enough for now.

She was beat; she usually put in more hours than this staying later on weekend nights. Maybe it was the worry and upset over the water pipe. She felt as if she'd worked two twelve-hour shifts back to back.

But the moment she stepped outside and locked the back door, she saw her journey wasn't going to be an easy one. She still had to remove the snow coating her SUV and chip away at the ice frozen solid to the windows before she could even think about trying to drive. And once she was on her way, the roads would be more than a challenge.

Twenty minutes later, falling snow pelted her trusty Jeep with big wet flakes, and it was impossible to see more than a few inches in front of her. The accumulation on the road was sloppy and tricky to drive in. It caught at the wheels and tossed the vehicle every which way, so she slowed to a crawl to navigate through the town streets and along the county road where other vehicles' tires had mashed the mire down into an icy compact crust.

When she turned off onto the private road, she relaxed a bit. Almost home. The evergreens and cottonwoods lining the lane were bent low from the heavy snow and scraped at the top of her Jeep; that's when it got tough going. She fought the wheel to stay on the narrow road.

Only two other sets of tire tracks marked the way in the otherwise absolute darkness. One set, which was almost snow filled, veered off down a long, tree-lined drive. Evan Thornton's place. The remaining tracks had to be her son's and led her a few more miles into the hills, up her driveway and into the shelter of her garage.

Thank heaven. She was home and in one piece, and not that much worse for wear. Lights flicked on and there was Alex, holding open the inside door, already in a flannel T-shirt and pants she'd gotten him for Christmas. His blond hair was rumpled and in serious need of a cut. His dog panted at his side. "Hey, Mom. I was just nuking some cocoa. Want some?"

"Are you kidding? I'd love a cup."

"Cool." He flashed her a quick grin and disappeared behind the door, the dog, Max, loping along after him.

As she gave the door a shove, her back popped. Great. That was going to be the next disaster. Her back was going to go out. Every joint she owned creaked. *Wasn't life eventually supposed to be easier, Lord? Or are You trying to tell me something?*

She rescued her purse from the floor, along with the small paper sack with the last two cinnamon rolls. She had to wonder, as she elbowed through the door and into the laundry room, whether God was sending her a sign.

Every time she tried to get ready to sell the diner for good something happened to hold her firmly here. In the last six months, her sister Rachel had married and moved away, the roof had needed to be replaced and now the plumbing. Those repairs would erode a big chunk of the savings she'd been squirreling away. Not good.

Then again, it was never a true disaster, either. The Lord might be trying to tell her something, but He always made sure she had help, too. The image of Evan Thornton flashed into her mind. Tall, broad-shouldered, he had the kind of quiet strength that made a woman sigh and wish—even a woman like her who did not place any faith in the non-constant nature of men.

Sure, some men were constant, but it was a rare thing. The trouble was, it would be easy to start believing Evan was one of those kind of men. He'd helped out tonight without expecting more than a thank-you. And what was it he'd said? *Glad I could make a difference.* He had his heart in the right place. Why had it seemed that he was so sad? Not depressed-sad, just…lonely-sad. He hadn't wanted to go home to an empty house.

It hit her the moment she saw her strapping son at the microwave, punching the buttons. Hadn't

Evan's youngest boy, who was a year older than Alex, gone to college this year? Maybe that's why he seemed so lonely.

Alex's crooked grin lit up his face. "Excellent, Mom. Sit down, take a load off. Want me to get that for you?"

He could have been a young, hip butler for the attention he was giving her. And while it was nice, she had to wonder what was behind his very sweet behavior. She let him take her purse, the dinner sack and her keys and then watched in amazement while he set them on the counter. He couldn't resist peeking into the sack.

"Sweet. Good call. I could use a cinnamon roll. I'm a growing boy, you know."

"I've noticed."

"Here, sit down." His hand on her elbow guided her to one of the chairs at the breakfast bar.

"Okay, what's up?" What trouble are you in now? She bit her tongue before she said it. "This is bringing to mind the time you drove into the school bus in the school parking lot and backed up traffic for thirty minutes."

"My dearest mother, now why would I be up to anything? I'm a good kid."

"*Good* is a relative term." He *was* a good boy; her heart swelled up with endless love for him, but he was a teenage boy, no matter how great a kid he was, and he needed constant vigilant guidance. Even if she was proud of the fine man he was growing up to be.

As he fetched the full steaming mug he'd obviously fixed before she'd stepped through the door, she watched him like a hawk, trying to ferret out a clue to the truth. But nothing. No hint.

She kept staring at him, but he wasn't going to crack. She took the mug he slid across the counter to her. "Okay, spill it. I want the truth."

All innocence, he opened the microwave door. "There's no truth. I just thought I'd be nice to my mom."

"I like it. I just need to know why."

"Well, let me think. I did rob a bank tonight, and I stopped by a convenience store and robbed that, too." He laughed at his own joke. "Am I funny or what?"

"Hilarious." Paige took a sip of chocolate. That hit the spot. She eyed her son over the rim of the cup. This was a teenaged boy, home from his date with a girl she didn't approve of, and home early, despite the weather, come to think of it.

A sudden panic began to lick through her soul. He hadn't gotten into some serious trouble with his girlfriend, had he? She'd been sure to talk to him about his responsibilities toward Beth, to respect her, but— *No,* she couldn't begin to think about that!

Alex hopped onto the stool beside her. "Yo, don't

have a heart attack or nothin'. You don't think I really robbed some place? I was just yanking your chain. It's my job to torment my mom." He grinned, knowing he was perfectly adorable.

"Just like it's my job to worry and make sure you grow up right."

"I'm growing up right." He rolled his eyes. "All I did was take Beth home after the movie. That's it."

Oh, maybe they broke up. Maybe that's what this was about. He was home early, making hot chocolate and sitting next to her. Maybe he wanted to talk. Relief rushed through her. "How is Beth?"

"Okay. I met her mom." He shrugged, leaving her to wait while he rammed a cinnamon roll into his mouth, bit off a huge chunk and chewed.

Beth's mom? That wasn't what Paige expected him to say. Had the woman said something to upset him? She took a sip of the steaming cocoa and licked the marshmallow froth off her lip, waiting for the rest of the tale.

Finally, after a long beat of silence, Alex confessed. "I took Beth up to the door, and her mom was waiting. She was drunk, I think. And she started chewing out Beth, and I just…" He swallowed hard. "Felt so bad for her."

"Me, too." Paige knew Beth's mom worked at the local motel as a cleaning lady, and rumor had it she was a woman with a sad life.

"Beth didn't want me to see her mom like that, so she wanted me to go. But she said something to me." He hung his head. "That I was lucky. To have you for a mom. And she's right." He attacked the cinnamon roll again.

Paige let the impact of his words settle. Her heart gave another tug. "You're a pretty great kid, too, you know. I got lucky when the angels gave me you."

"I know. I am a good kid." There was that look again, The Eye, the one that made it impossible for her not to melt with adoration for him. He shoved off the counter, taking the cinnamon roll with him. "I got youth group stuff tomorrow. Did ya need help at the diner?"

"No, we'll manage without you."

"It'll be hard, I know." He was gone, bounding through the house, thumping and thudding as he went down the hall and into the basement where his bedroom was.

Leaving her alone. The warmth of the house, of her home, surrounded her as she sipped her cocoa. Alex's advanced calculus and physics textbooks were stacked on the table, ready for him to do his homework when he caught a chance over the weekend. On the counter next to the microwave was the admission booklet and information from the college he'd be attending in the fall.

High-school graduation was just around the corner, in the last week of May, and then Alex would be getting ready to leave home. She'd be putting the diner up for sale and then she'd have all the time in the world to follow her own dreams. Paige had been planning for this time of her life for a long while. She deeply wanted this new future rushing toward her.

But maybe she wasn't in so much of a hurry to get there.

She finished her hot chocolate, let the peace of the night settle around her and remembered to give thanks for all the good things in her life.

## Chapter Four

Too much time on his hands. At first Evan had filled the void of the weekends with work on Saturday and church on Sunday, but the truth was, he worked long enough hours during the week and he'd more than caught up on his work load, which was usually such that he was always struggling to keep up. Now, suddenly, he was caught-up. After six months of working most weekends, he had no reason to be at the office. And so he was wandering around the local feed store, looking at stuff he didn't need. At loose ends.

"Getting ready for summer camping?" Dalton Whitely had inherited the store from his granddad, and had been several years behind Evan in school. Even though they'd played in sports together for a year, when Evan was a senior and Dalton a freshman, Evan really only knew the man as a salesman.

Now that his life was slowing down, Evan was noticing he had a lot of acquaintances, folks he knew by name, but not nearly enough true friends. He wasn't sure what that said about him, but he knew he was guilty of keeping a healthy distance between him and most people. He'd turned into a man who didn't trust easily. Maybe, when that came to trusting a wife, that was a good thing. But he felt adrift these days. Unconnected. The flier he'd kept, the one about the Bible study, popped into his mind again.

Maybe, he thought. Maybe it was just the thing he needed. He realized Dalton was waiting for an answer. "I'm just looking. Don't need a new tent, but those are sure nice."

"Latest models. Just put 'em out." Dalton flashed a cordial smile. "You let me know if you have any questions?"

"Yep." Looking at the camping gear reminded him of better times. Maybe he'd like camping alone. It was something he'd never done before. For more summers than he could count, he and the boys had spent most weekends up in the mountains: camping, hiking, fishing, hunting. There was nothing like riding up into the mountains on horseback. It was like stepping back a century in time. He hadn't thought about the summer to come. He was already dreading it.

As he turned his back on the brand-new pup tents

and eyed the wall of bright halters and braided bridles, he already knew how the summer was going to go. Cal would be off working to make spending money and money for books for next year; he'd probably go off with Blake and fight fires all summer. A good paying job, great for the boys, but Evan was going to be alone. He'd have to face the prospect of a long summer by himself.

His cell buzzed in his jacket pocket. He fished it out, hope springing eternal as he glanced at the screen. It was neither of his sons, but he was grinning as he answered. "Hi, Phil."

"Hey, I wanted to thank you for the business last night. Things are slow and I needed the work."

"Great. I hope you gave her a good price. Paige seems like a nice lady."

That was an understatement. Evan had thought of her on and off all morning, since she'd slipped cinnamon rolls in with his pie, and he'd had them with his coffee this morning. He couldn't get the image of her out of his mind, the softness she was so careful to hide. He'd been trying not to think of her, but things kept happening to bring his mind back to her. The cinnamon rolls, the sight of the diner as he drove past and now Phil's call. That unsettled tightness clamped back around his chest, and he didn't like it. He tried to will it away, but it remained.

"Seems. You mean you don't know?"

Okay, Phil was fishing for the truth. What truth? There was nothing between him and Paige. How crazy was that? And Phil *knew* Evan's position on women, including all the reasons behind it. Phil had been with him through the aftermath of the divorce. "I can't believe you! I don't have a personal interest in Paige. I was eating dinner in the diner when the pipe burst. That's it."

"Oh. Well, that explains it then. For a minute there, I thought you just might have found a woman who could help you get over what Liz did to you."

"You sound disappointed."

"I am, but I understand. I'm on my way into town right now."

"Here? You're coming here?" For some reason that was too much of a switch for his thoughts to take. Probably because they were still lagging, as he gazed out the store's window at the front window of Paige's diner. He realized he had a new halter and lead rope in hand, although he didn't remember picking one out, and he headed to the cash stand. "What's the deal? You're not out in this neck of the woods much, not since Cal flew the coop."

"I started work on an estimate for the diner, and realized I had to come take a second look to do it up right. I need the business, so I want to do a good job. You wouldn't want to give Paige a good word or two about me, huh? She looks savvy enough to get more than a few estimates for me to compete with. What do you say?"

"I say come meet me for lunch and I'll let you talk me into it. Or at least, you can talk to her about it."

"Done. I'm, uh, about five minutes away. I'll meet you at the diner?"

Evan pocketed his phone and set his purchases on the scarred wooden counter as Dalton slid behind to run the decades-old cash register. Funny thing how he had a better view of the diner from here. And he could see not only the diner, but also the woman who ran it, out salting down the freshly shoveled sidewalk in front of the door.

She looked as lovely as the day's sunshine. She wore a bright yellow spring coat over her standard dark sweater and jeans, and he couldn't remember ever noticing her in a bright color before. If he had, surely he would have taken a long second look. The splash of color brought out the pale rosebud pink of her cheeks, and the sheen of golden highlights in her dark brown hair. Teenagers climbed out of a minivan, calling out to her, and she greeted them with an unguarded smile.

The impact hit him like a punch to his chest.

"Should I just put that on your bill, Evan?" Dalton asked.

"Uh…yep." Rattled but not wanting to show it, Evan nodded thanks to the storeowner, grabbed his bagged purchase and walked on wooden legs to the doors. He was only distantly aware of pushing through the swinging door and into the chill of the wind. Cold penetrated his shirt, for he hadn't zipped his jacket, but it registered only vaguely. He could not seem to take his eyes off Paige.

She was talking with the kids, listening attentively, her head tipped slightly to the left, her thick fall of bangs cascading over her forehead. She was pretty. She was nice. She was a good mom. That was easy to see as her son stood at her side, tall and good-natured; Evan remembered that Alex McKaslin had played on both the football and basketball teams with Cal. He was a good kid. And Paige, as busy as she was, had made it to every game, home and away. A longing filled him as he inexplicably felt drawn to her, and suddenly the distance between them seemed intolerable.

What was happening to him? You're lonely, man, he admonished himself. And loneliness was wearing on him. Making him vulnerable. Making him wish for what he knew was impossible. For what he never wanted to try again. Marriage had been a miserable path for both him and Liz: even though he'd tried his best to make her happy, he'd failed.

It wasn't all his fault—he took what blame was his and he'd learned from it, but she'd been a hard woman to please. Selfish to the core, and in leaving she had ruined his credit and nearly bankrupted him, holding the custody of the boys over him. That's what he should be reminding himself of every time he looked at Paige McKaslin.

Except it was hard, and he didn't know why the memory of the disasters and hurts of his past weren't keeping his interest in her at bay. Paige was talking with the teenagers now, easy and open. Her son and the other kids seemed to like her so well. She ushered them inside, holding the small plastic bag of rock salt in the crook of one arm. When she stepped through the threshold and out of sight, it was as if the sun had slipped behind a cloud, and he shivered.

"Evan! Earth to Evan! Are you all right, man?"

Evan realized he'd been staring across the street as though he was mesmerized. He shook his head, clearing his thoughts, and looked around. His big burly brother-in-law was bounding down the sidewalk, his plumber's van parked six or seven car lengths up the street. He realized Phil must have called his name several times. *Do I look like a fool, or what?*

Not knowing what to do with himself, he yanked open the passenger door of his truck and tossed the bag on the floor. "Phil. You look ready to work."

"I came to get a better look in the crawl space. Didn't want to wear my Sunday best." Phil was no dim bulb. There was a knowing twinkle in his eyes as he gazed across the street. "That Paige McKaslin sure is a nice lady, don't you think?"

That sounded like a loaded question. Just how long had he been watching Paige? And how transparent had he been? "She seems nice enough. She runs a good business. Serves some of the best food in the county."

"All good reasons to go get something to eat at her place, right?" Phil seemed to take that in stride.

As Evan stepped off the curb, he realized that maybe he'd been misreading Phil's statements. He was starting to scare himself. But considering the financial devastation a woman had brought to his life, he probably *should* be terrified. He was committed to being totally single. That was the way of it. Nothing was going to change his mind about that. "I'm in the mood for some good homemade chili."

"Homemade chili?"

"It's her family's recipe. Her parents and her grandparents. It's good stuff."

"Now you've got me hungry. How are the boys?"

"Do you think I know? Good, I guess. They're busy. You just wait. Has your daughter picked a college yet?"

"She's got another year, thank the Lord, but that'll go by quick. Then Marie and I won't know what to do with ourselves." Phil hiked up onto the sidewalk, his toolbox rattling. He seemed nonchalant about the upcoming change in his life—as if it would be an easy transition.

Not so easy. Then again, Phil had a good wife. A woman who'd stood by him and worked beside him every day of their marriage. An empty nest might not be so empty in the presence of a happy marriage. But a happy marriage—those had to be rare. It certainly hadn't happened for him.

"Hi, Mr. Thornton. Welcome back." One of Paige's teenage twin cousins cracked her gum and pulled out two menus. "Wherever you wanna sit. You just go ahead and pick."

"Thanks. You might want to let Paige know that the plumber is back with some questions."

"Oh, yeah, like, I'll go get her." The teenager accompanied them down the aisle. "Paige is having a day." She rolled her eyes. "So it'll probably be a minute or two before she's free."

Evan remembered what Cal had called the Mc-Kaslin twins, who were a year behind him in school: A hundred percent clueless, but they get your order right. He'd suspected Cal had a crush on one of them—he wasn't sure if it was this one, since the girls were entirely identical right down to their hair styles and jewelry.

Evan chose a booth in the back away from the crowd of teenagers that had settled into two booths near the front. He recognized most of them from the church's youth group. Cal had been active in it up until he'd left home.

Evan opened the menu as a formality, mostly to give him a moment or two to develop a plan. Paige McKaslin had blown him away last night, and he hadn't expected that. And today when he'd seen that private side of her, it had been something he'd never seen in her before last night. What would he do if last night had changed things between them?

"I'm gonna get the chili, too. It's cold out there, and it comes with a side of cornbread. I'm a sucker for cornbread." Phil snapped the menu shut. "Oh, here she comes. Hi, Paige."

"Gentlemen." There was no falter in her step and no flaw in her collected manner as she approached their table. "Phil, I'm told you have some questions. What can I do for you?"

"I need to take another look down below. And where's your hot-water tank?"

"Off the kitchen. Eat first, then flag me down and I'll show you what you need." She slipped two water glasses onto the table. "What can I get you two?"

Evan realized he was staring at her again. "Paige, you remember Phil?"

"Uh, of course I do. Phil, Evan braved the dark reaches of the crawl space to turn off the water for me."

"He did, huh? I wondered how a skinny thing

like you could manage to turn that valve. It about gave me a hernia when I went to turn it back on."

Paige laughed; she liked the plumber. She liked that he was here to do the estimate the right way, and she liked that he was a friend of Evan's. "You two wanted to order?"

"You know where I'm going," Evan accused her. "And I'm not ordering until we come to an agreement."

"You're going to charge me for your plumbing work last night?"

"No, ma'am. I don't want you thinking you're going to give me a free meal. You charge me like any other customer, or I take my business down the street to your competitor."

"Ouch, you drive a hard bargain, but if you're going to call me 'ma'am,' then I'm going to insist you go down the street to my competition. I just am not going to put up with anyone reminding me how old I am. I'm just not going to do it."

Evan chuckled, leaning back in the booth just enough that the sunshine streaming through the slatted blinds washed over him, haloing him in light. "I think we have ourselves a bargain. I'll have a large bowl of your famous chili, miss."

"Miss. I like that." Her face felt hot; she wanted to blame it on the sunshine, but she knew that wasn't the cause at all. She felt as if she were blushing; the good Lord knew she felt *younger.* She couldn't really explain it, but she didn't like it, and she took a step back. "How about you, Phil?"

"Make that two."

"You've got it. I'll be right back with your cornbread. Excuse me." She didn't even look at Evan as she pounded away, quick to turn her mind to the new party crowding through the doorway and the teenagers getting restless in the booths.

But as she took the kids' orders, Evan remained in the corner of her vision. She could not shake the memory of his confession last night of how he'd been in no hurry to head home to an empty house.

Her son gave her a cheeky grin as he ordered two monster burgers and extra fries, and she felt a hard pang of sympathy for the man when she realized his sons were no longer at home.

Sympathy—not interest—she told herself firmly. She felt sympathy for the man. Maybe because she was going to be in his shoes before long. As she clipped the order to the wheel, she caught sight of Alex sitting in the booth with his friends. Beth was with him today, crowded against his side, a quiet, blue-eyed redhead who had ordered a cheeseburger in a polite voice. Remembering Alex's confession last night about Beth's mom, she had a harder time not approving of the girl.

"Paige?" Her younger sister, Amy, caught her attention through the pass-through window. "Uh…could you come back here for a minute?"

Paige's heart caught. "Are you all right? You're as pale as a sheet."

"I, uh, you're gonna have to take over the grill. I'm feeling sick." With a clatter, Amy suddenly dropped the spatula she held and dashed off at a run.

Okay, that's not good. Wanting to run after her sister, and knowing the food sizzling on the grill needed to be tended to, she hurried around into the back. She snatched up the spatula and flipped burgers and rescued a batch of chicken tenders from the deep fryer. Wasn't it just her luck that she could see Evan Thornton through the window? She had a perfect view of him, and with the way the sunshine poured through window highlighting him, it was like a sign from heaven.

*I know what you're trying to tell me, Lord.* The realization hit her like a sunbeam. Evan had become a more frequent customer over the winter. He was like so many of her other regulars, the ones who came alone, as often as not because they needed more than a meal. Friendship. Connection. Fellowship.

All her life, she'd been the one looking after others. First as the big sister taking care of her brother and younger sisters. Then as the adult in the family, after their parents' deaths. Finally she became a mom, and the role of caretaking just became hers through the years.

Heaven knew she was more parent than cousin to the twins, who were so lost, what with the way their parents lived. Somehow, her diner had become a big family kitchen in a way. And while her thoughts drifted down the hall as she wondered if Amy was okay, she quickly built the bacon, cheese and chili burgers for table eight, and held off on the incoming orders so she could run down to check on her sister.

"Order up," she called to Brianna who was just back from seating the last of the incoming customers.

"Is Amy, like, okay?" Concern wreathed the girl's face.

"I'm just going to go check on her. You'll watch the front for me?"

"Yeah, totally!"

"Thanks, sweetie." Paige started down the hall and found Amy washing her face at the sink in the women's bathroom. The way she clung to the edge of the basin told Paige everything. She caught Amy's reflection in the mirror, grabbed a length of paper towel from the dispenser and held it out to her. "I would say you've got a stomach bug, but something tells me that's not your problem."

Amy let out a watery sigh as she grabbed the

paper and swiped it over her face. "I'm almost afraid to let myself think it, in case this is just an upset stomach."

"Does your new husband know about this?"

Amy's eyes filled. "This is only the second morning I've felt like this, and well, I think it's too early to take a pregnancy test."

"I'll run across the street to the drug store and get one, and we can read the instructions to see. Or, wait, no, you want to share this with your husband."

"I do."

"Whatever you need, sweetie."

The diamond wedding set on Amy's left hand caught the light, sparkling like a brand-new shiny promise. Life had been hard for Amy for a long time. She'd been a rebellious teenager, and unhappy trapped in this small town. She'd run away her senior year in high school for a bigger and more exciting life in a big city, but she'd returned unhappy and disillusioned with her baby son in her arms.

She'd worked so hard all the years since to raise her son and provide for him, and now Paige prayed for her nightly—that this new marriage and the man in her life were everything she deserved, that her road ahead would be easier and filled with love—the kind of love that could last.

"Thank you, Paige. You are the best big sister."

"No, I'm just marginal and very lucky to have

you. Why don't you sit down for a bit? I'll get some ginger ale and crackers to calm your stomach. Sound like a good idea?"

"No, because the lunch rush is about to hit."

"Not your problem. It's mine."

Amy wadded up the towel and gave it a toss. It landed neat as a pin in the wastebasket. Her heart-shaped face was ashen, but her jeweled eyes were big and bright and full of hope. "I'm not sick, I don't think, and I want to finish my shift."

"Not on your life. You're going home. First you're going to sit until you're looking better and when you are, we'll discuss you staying at the diner. C'mon, baby sister." Paige put her arm around Amy's slender shoulders. "You come let me take care of you."

"I'm not sick."

"Then you're something better, and you need to take care. C'mon." She navigated them through the door and down the hall. "Go sit and I'll be right out."

"But the lunch rush—"

"Go!" Paige softened her stern tone with a smile. "Brandilyn," she called to the teen, who was standing at the till, her forehead wrinkled in concentration as she stared at the ticket and then the cash register keys. "Brandilyn, honey, go fetch two orders of cornbread for Mr. Thornton's table. I'll grab Alex to man the till."

"Like, I totally need help!"

Paige rang up the ticket, handed the change back to Mrs. Brisbane, and thanked her for coming. It took a second to haul Alex from his friends, he came with only a half-hearted complaint, and took over front-desk duties so she could go catch up in the kitchen. She ladled out two huge bowls of chili for Evan and the plumber, and started a row of burgers on the grill. After swiping off her hands, she brought Amy a bowl of crackers and a big cup of soda. Amy looked too miserable to tackle the crackers but sipped at the pop with a look of deep gratitude.

Since Alex was answering the diner's phone, probably for a take-out order, she grabbed her cell from her pocket and dialed Amy's home number. It took only a moment to let Heath know what was going on, and before she knew it, the meat patties were done. She dressed the buns, plated the meals, added a heaping round of golden fries and rang the bell.

Out of the corner of her eye, she caught sight of Evan, digging into his chili and talking animatedly with Phil. There was something about him, something nice.

What was she thinking? She filled a basket with raw cut potatoes and lowered it into the fryer. She was *so* not interested in Evan Thornton. In any man. She didn't have time for one. Room for one. Heart

for one. Her life was far too full taking care of everyone else. And that was besides the fact that she'd had
enough of men. One husband was more than enough
for any woman. What would she want with another?

More customers were piling in, Alex was seating
them, and she turned to dress two lunch salads at the
counter to go with the club sandwich for table
twelve. Heath came in through the back, Brandilyn
rushed in to grab the green salads and rushed right
back out again, and more orders filled the wheel.

She had enough to do to fill two lifetimes. She
didn't have time to waste on romance. She was just
too busy for impossible dreams.

## *Chapter Five*

Evan scraped the last bite of chili from the bottom of the oversized bowl and licked it off the spoon. He was near to bursting, but Paige's chili had really hit the spot today. The sun had vanished and ice pellets were pounding the window next to him, dampening the lunch rush. The traffic along the main street was thinning.

It was easier to look out the window than to look around. He knew he'd catch sight of Paige hurrying between the kitchen and the front, checking on the waitresses and running the till, for she'd let her son rejoin his friends in the booth.

When she was around, his gaze kept finding her. And that was the kind of thing Phil had noticed.

Phil gave his plate a shove and leaned against the padded back of the booth. "You're right. That was the best bowl of chili I've had since I was stationed in Texas. Say, did you know we heard from Liz the other day?"

"I thought you vowed to never talk to her again." Just like me, he thought.

"She called right in the middle of supper. Marie thought it was a telemarketer and almost unplugged the phone. Should have done it, and we would have, too, if we'd known it was her. She's in Tucson."

*I don't want to hear this.* Evan's guts tightened. The only thing Liz ever brought him was bad memories and deep emotional pain. "I know she's your sister, but I don't want to talk about her. She took what she wanted." And how. But he got what mattered, the real treasures, the real riches. Their boys. "You wanted to work on your estimate for Paige? She looks a little less busy."

"I can take a hint. I only meant to say that Liz couldn't rise to the challenge. She didn't grow up all the way. But that doesn't mean all women are like that. Look at my Marie. There isn't a better gem in all the world."

Evan's guts twisted hard with an old, bitter pain. Some losses ran too deep. Some wounds left a vicious scar. "Look, I don't need this, Phil. I've got time on my hands with both boys gone. I admit it. But I don't want to hear it one more time. A woman isn't going to be the answer. I'm better off alone."

"No one is better off alone. God didn't make us that way. That's all I'm gonna say, and well, I've got one more thing. Marie knows this real nice lady from her Bible study. Smart, kind, has a good job. Her husband passed on a few years ago from cancer. She's a good kind of woman. We could have her over for dinner, and you, too—"

Phil meant well. There was no doubt about that. But Phil had a great wife. A woman he'd always been able to count on. A woman who did her best never to let him down.

How could he understand what it was like never to have had that? To have finally finished up the last of his scheduled payments on the nearly fifty-thousand-dollar credit-card debt his wife had left him with.

Then there had been the legal battles, the settlement he'd made in order to keep the boys…everything. If that was the way a woman who said she loved him treated her husband, then he wanted nothing to do with that again.

The trouble was, and he'd known for a long time, that not all women were made like Liz. The truth was, he just didn't think he had the heart to try again.

His gaze found Paige as she swept down the aisle with her lean, quick efficiency. She looked spare and stern and very in charge, but her manner didn't fool him; it was the same as the black sweater she wore. The color was severe, but superficial. He didn't know why last night's single glance beneath Paige's daily armor made him want to like her.

He didn't want to like any woman, right? "I'm not interested, Phil. But I appreciate it. I know you mean well."

"Mean well? What do you mean? We're more like brothers, that's how I see you. And the boys, they're my nephews. You know how I feel about 'em. Our kids have always been close, the way cousins ought to be.

"But you know what? After a hard day's work, a good day's work, I go home to Marie. She lights up when I walk through the door. Now everything's right, she says and everything just fades into the background. I started thinkin' last night how you go home to an empty house. You've got no Marie."

Evan wanted to tell Phil that he sure wished he'd been as lucky as to have a woman like Marie in the first place, but his throat tightened with a strange aching emotion. The cynical part of him that had been hurt so hard and deep wanted to say how he was glad to be single and unencumbered by a woman who would only hurt him.

But the truth was, he was not that bitter. Not wholly. Phil was truly blessed, and that's what Evan couldn't say. What made his throat sear with emotion had nothing to do with bitterness and everything to do with a sorrow he couldn't quite explain. At least Phil knew how fortunate he was. At least he knew the value of a good woman and appreciated the difference she made in his life.

He thought of the empty house waiting for him. It wasn't the boys that had made his house a home, he knew, although they had filled it with a joy and chaos that was as equally wonderful. Finally, he found his voice, but it didn't sound at all like his, as his words came thick and gruff. "You're very lucky you have your wife. Anyone can see you got a good woman."

"Then you can see how it is. Life is about the choices we make, about doing the right thing that's asked of us or doing the easy thing. You got a bum wrap when Liz treated you the way she did, no doubt about that, but you can see that there are good women out there. Women who are alone, and who have a lot of heart to give a man. Maybe one woman who would make you happy."

"Happy. That sounds nice."

I'm not about to trust another woman just to find out. Not that he could admit that in a public place or anywhere. There was no way to really know a person, no way to peer into the future and see what choices they would make—to stay committed, to stay devoted, to stay….period.

How did he admit, even to himself, that part of

the emptiness of his current life was that he had no one to share it with. No one to come home to and take care of and care for. Being a father had met those needs close enough that he didn't miss the primary relationship of marriage…not too much, anyway. Being a single father was a whole world better than how unhappy both he and Liz had made one another.

But it was hard not to notice the married couples in the diner. Men and women his age, with kids crowding into the booth with them or without, having sneaked away for a lunch alone, and it was a reminder that some marriages did last. That there were a lot of faithful, loyal, good women out there.

But knowing it and trusting it were two different things.

"Well, that's all I'm gonna say on the subject." Phil pushed his way out of the booth. "You want to wait around? I'm not gonna be long. Marie would love to have you over to supper."

"Sounds good, but I've got plans."

"Not plans with a lady?"

"As Cal would say, 'no-oo way.' I'm going to catch a movie, but I'll wait for you. Paige is a nice lady, so you're giving her a good deal, right?"

"She's a very nice lady." Phil's grin was mischievous as he backed away. "I'll do well by her, don't you worry."

Mischievous? No, Phil had jumped to the wrong conclusions, but that was okay. Evan leaned across the aisle to take the morning's paper left on an unoccupied table. He checked the baseball scores and then the local news and tried hard not to notice Paige McKaslin from the corner of his eye.

Not that he was interested, of course. She was at the front, ringing up the teenagers' orders, giving them a serious discount by the sounds of things, as the kids chorused their thanks and clamored out the door.

An icy wind skiffed down the aisle and he shivered. It felt like snow.

"Crazy weather, isn't it?" Paige had a hot cup of coffee and set it on his table. Along with his meal ticket. "As promised. Is there anything else I can get you?"

"Nope. The chili was excellent. It always is."

"Why thanks. It seemed like a good special to run what with winter thinking it can make a comeback. You just take your time here."

"I noticed your son earlier. Seems he managed last night out there driving."

She flushed. "I'm a worrier, I admit it. Lord knows I try to control it, but it gets the best of me. He's out there driving right now and it's snowing. Look at that. It's the last day of April and coming down like it's December.

"What about your boys? Do they make it home much for the weekends?"

Evan stared at the white slash of snow veiling the world that had been promising a sunny spring. Somehow, the snow keeping things frozen and isolated seemed appropriate. "You know how busy they get."

"I already do." Understanding gleamed warm and rare in her eyes as blue as a spring sky, and she set the coffee carafe on the corner of the table, a deliberate movement, as if she had something to say on the matter. "Alex isn't even gone from home yet, and he's so busy he might as well be. The youth group this morning, off with his girlfriend this afternoon. They're going to the mall and then the Young Life night at the church. I'm catering their supper."

"If I remember right, your diner does a lot of catering for our church events."

"I do what I can." She shrugged a slender shoulder, the movement drawing his gaze to the elegant grace of her movements as she crossed her arms around her middle and gazed out the window in the direction of the main road through town, as if her thoughts were firmly with her son. "I don't think I'll know what to do with all the peace and quiet once he's on his own, and that will be too bad, because I've gotten to like the chaos."

She was gently teasing, he realized, his throat

strangely aching again with emotions that he, like her, did not want to reveal. "Believe me, the quiet isn't as nice as the chaos."

"I was afraid you were going to say that. You've confirmed what I've already guessed."

It was the way she confessed that, with a genuine flash of what looked like both regret and a mother's deep love. Maybe that's what hooked him like a fish on a line and tugged him so hard through the current of his own wounds that he wasn't prepared for the speed of it. He wasn't prepared at all.

He gaped at her, as if he couldn't breathe the air, seeing the truth in Paige McKaslin in a way he'd never had the time or the reason to before. She was the woman who'd stayed when her husband left, everyone in town knew the story. She made a success of the diner with courtesy and hard work. She raised what appeared to be a great kid, and treated everyone she came across with courtesy and respect.

Why the words spilled over his tongue, he couldn't say, or where they came from, but he couldn't believe his own ears, even as he heard himself speak. "Say, you wouldn't happen to know about that Bible study over at the coffee shop on Wednesdays? I know it's hosted by a woman from our church."

"Sure. Katharine is my cousin—"

"I've been thinking about going—"

"You have?"

He paused. What was going on? Why was he trembling like a teenager asking a girl out on his first date?

He didn't want to date. He didn't want a woman, but he liked Paige. He couldn't seem to stop himself from asking the question. "Would you come with me?"

"Oh, uh, as a friendly face, you mean?" She seemed confused. Her eyebrows slanted and she took a step back. Her hands flew out and she grabbed the coffeepot as if to shield her heart with it.

Not what I should have asked, he realized too late. He was forty-two years old. What was he doing? He was too old to start again. Too set in his ways to think about dating. Too wounded to ever trust another woman intimately.

He *could* take the chicken's way out and agree, to say, sure, that's what he wanted, a friendly face at the meeting. He could save himself a lot of embarrassment and risk to his heart if he just corrected his impulsive question with a simple nod.

But it wasn't the truth. Not at all. "No," he said in a choked voice, while the little voice in his head kept telling him to get up and run and never come back. "I meant would you go with me. As, a, well, as a d-date."

Too late to take the words back, he watched the

confusion slide from her lovely face. Horror widened her eyes. Big mistake, Thornton, he thought, surprised that the main thing he felt was remorse instead of relief. It made no sense, but it told him something. He admired Paige McKaslin. He liked a lot of things about her. It hurt to admit, but the truth was the truth.

She's going to say no. Evan saw the answer on her face. And how she bit her bottom lip as she figured out how to turn him down.

Maybe he would save her the trouble. "Hey, it's okay. I don't know why I just blurted that out. I haven't been on a date in over twenty years."

"Me, either." The tension lines around her mouth eased. "That's hysterical. Twenty years. That's a long time to be out of it. I just don't date, Evan, I'm sorry."

"I understand." He didn't meet her gaze but turned toward the window where a vigorous snowfall bordered on whiteout conditions. "We're going to need a snowplow to get home before long if this keeps up. I'd better go while the getting's good."

Somehow her feet weren't taking her up the aisle, like they were supposed to. Maybe it was shock rooting her to the same spot on the floor. Evan Thornton had asked her out? That didn't seem right. No one had asked her out in all the years since her husband had left. She always figured the reason was simple: Jimmy had always told her she was a simple small-town girl, nothing special, but a hard-working salt-of-the-earth type.

Not exactly the kind of woman men lined up to date and fall in love with, no.

As she caught her reflection in the window glass, she saw a woman whose face was too long, her nose a little too big, with a few too many character lines to be thought of as pretty.

Evan seemed embarrassed as he kept his attention riveted on the storm. The floor let go of her feet, and woodenly she stumbled down the aisle and away to the safety of the kitchen.

Brandilyn swung through the door with a full basin of dirties. She strained as if she were carrying a thousand pounds. With a groan, she unloaded the tub onto the sink counter. "So, Paige, is Mr. Thornton, like, totally cool, well, for an old guy?"

Paige leaned to the side to bring Evan in focus through the order-up window. Yeah, totally cool, to use the teenager's phrase.

But not "cool" the way Brandilyn probably meant it. Cool, in Paige's opinion, because he was the kind of man who stayed. He'd been the one to pick up the pieces when his marriage failed. He raised his boys, made them a good home. He'd provided for them and gave them a good head start in the world.

He was a nice man, handsome, strong, capable

and with those wide shoulders of his, he could make a woman, even one as jaded as she, wish . . .just a little in absolutely impossible dreams.

And how foolish was that? "After you run a load of dishes, could you start prepping salads? If this weather keeps up, we're going to be dead tonight, so if you want to go early, it would be okay."

"Like, who wants to work?" The girl pitched her voice over the chink and clang of the dishes as she unloaded the bin. "But I really need the hours. Like super bad."

"Then how do you feel about managing the front tonight?"

"You mean it?" A cup crashed into the top rack as Brandilyn spun around, forgetting what she was doing, excitement lighting her up. "That'd be so sweet! Like, I can do it. I know I can. Well, except for the cash register. But I'm catching on. Really, I am."

"I know, sweetie. You're doing great. You get better every week."

"Ya think so?"

The girl brightened so much, Paige saw all of Brandilyn's potential. The teenager was so bright, when she applied herself. She only had to figure that out. "I do. Did you get your registration notice from the community college yet?"

"It came and now Bree and I have to figure out what to take. It's totally weird."

"Did you want to bring your stuff by and we can go over it?"

"That'd be so awesome." Brandilyn put all her youthful energy into stacking the dishes into the industrial washer. "So, like, are you gonna go out with him?"

The fryer-basket handle slipped from Paige's fingers and plunged back into the sizzling hot oil. She jumped back in time to avoid getting burned, but she had the distinct impression she wasn't going to avoid getting burned in a metaphorical sense. The twins had overheard Evan. How many others had?

As if thinking of him had made him materialize before her eyes, her gaze found him. A six-foot-plus flesh-and-blood man, solid and substantial and everything that could possibly be good in a male human being, and something deep within her sighed at the sight of him standing in the threshold. That sigh was absolutely something she did not want to admit she felt, especially to herself.

"You're busy." His molasses-dark gaze roamed over her like a touch. "I'll just leave this on the counter by the till, okay?"

Her gaze slid to the ticket and the twenty-dollar bill in his hand. In his big, strong-looking hands that made her wonder what it would be like to feel that hand enclosed over hers. What would it be like to feel his wide palm against hers and his thick, tapered fingers twined through hers. Would she feel safe? Sheltered? Cherished?

There I go again, wishing for fairy tales. What was it about certain men that could affect a woman so foolishly? "I'll ring that up for you right now."

It was surprisingly hard to meet his gaze, and the moment their eyes connected he jerked away as if she'd slapped him. "I'll wait out here then."

And he was gone, big athletic strides that took him from her sight, That settled it. She *had* hurt his feelings. That was so far from what she'd intended. The surprise of his proposition still rocked her. Date? Her?

It was preposterous to think of dating at her age anyway. Ridiculous. Who would be interested in a woman with too much responsibility, too much work, and too many people to take care of? And no interests, no time for hobbies, let alone letting a man woo her into believing he loved her.

Hold it, your bitterness is showing. She cast a quick prayer of forgiveness heavenward. It was not easy trying to keep a clear heart in this world where men existed.

Oops, there it was again. In truth, she was a *little* bitter toward the male gender and although it had significantly faded over the years, as she'd gotten a better handle on it, it had not vanished completely.

She vowed to work harder on it as she caught sight of Evan waiting for her at the front counter.

He looked out the window. Gazed down the aisle. He looked at the award plaques from the local Better Business Bureau on the wall behind her. He looked everywhere but at her.

*Lord, I have hurt him.* She hadn't meant to, but what did she do now to fix this? She rang up the sale, counted back his change. But he held up his hand.

"Keep it." He looked straight ahead as he turned away. "See ya."

"Have a good day, Evan."

She watched the door swing shut, and she felt horrible. She'd been so stunned and confused she hadn't handled the situation right. She hated it when she made a mistake that hurt someone else, and she'd bungled this one but good.

This wasn't about the fact that Evan was a good customer. This was personal. She thought he was okay, for a man. Probably one of the most responsible men she knew, and responsibility was something she thought was a virtue in a man. He didn't deserve her rather cool response to him. He didn't deserve that kind of treatment at all.

And what if this stopped him from attending the Bible study? What if he'd been asking her so he wouldn't be going into a social situation alone, without a friendly face, and she'd blown that for him, too?

*I have to fix this. I have to make this right.* Somehow, someway, she vowed, telling herself it was her conscience that was troubling her.

And not her heart.

# Chapter Six

Evan shoveled the foot-high accumulation of wet, sloppy snow off his front walkway and grimaced as his back spasmed in protest. He'd leave the stuff to melt on its own, except that the local station had broken in to the baseball-game coverage to announce freezing temps and more snow expected overnight.

Yippee. He loved Montana weather...*not,* as Cal would say. With any luck, spring would return in full force soon and he could start planning that trip up into the foothills.

Until then, it looked as if he would spend the rest of the weekend snowed in.

*Good thing I stopped by the grocery store on the way home. It looked like he might be snowed in for a day or two.*

As he slipped the edge of the shovel under the

block of snow and heaved, humiliation rushed over him like the bite of the north wind. He'd needed something to do after leaving the diner. He'd called Phil on his cell to say he was going without explaining why he hadn't waited. He felt bad about that, but he'd fill him in the next time they were face to face.

What he felt even worse about was how he'd come on to Paige McKaslin like a teenager asking for his first date.

It wasn't just his inexperience with these matters. No, that wasn't what was eating him up inside. It was worse than that. It was that he hadn't even given it any forethought. Any planning. The question had just rolled impulsively off his tongue—and he didn't date! He didn't want to date. He planned on never dating again.

And, of course, the worst part of all was that she'd turned him down flat.

What was it she'd said? *That's hysterical* had been her exact words, and she'd looked as if she were trying not to laugh. She didn't date; okay, he could live with that. But he knew it wasn't the truth.

Why on earth didn't Paige date? She was a gorgeous, hardworking, together woman. Come to think of it, it was strange she'd never remarried. He knew the rumor was that her husband had had enough of her and run off, but that was gossip he'd accidentally

overheard around town years ago and he didn't believe it.

Not anymore, he figured, remembering the vulnerable woman he'd gotten to know last night

Unfortunately, that same Paige McKaslin didn't
seem to be available when he'd asked her out. The
professional, every-hair-in-place businesswoman
had shown up to say no.

He didn't feel put down or even put out. But his
chest was knotted up so tight and he couldn't explain
it. See why he'd given up dealing with women long
ago? See the kind of tangled mess they tied a reason-
able man up in?

He didn't want to admit that regret was building
up in him like the snow on the ground. Cold, and
growing colder, he gave the contents of the shovel a
good toss—and his back snapped, lightning-fast pain
searing down his back and into his left leg.

That can't be good. He didn't dare move. Not at
first. The pain was too searing. He took a few quick
breaths and tried moving the leg that wasn't wracked
with knifing pain. It made a fresh wave of agony ex-
plode in the small of his back. Great. What a treat to
be forty-two.

Then, suddenly, through the veil of snow, came
two golden beams of light. At first he thought it was
Blake's Jeep roaring up the snow-laden driveway,
but then he noticed it wasn't a black vehicle, but a

dark-green new model. It wasn't Phil; he drove a van, and Cal had that undependable sports car—

The light blinded him for a split second and then the SUV turned the last curve and slid to a graceful stop in the driveway. The porch lights shone on the window so he couldn't see whom was behind the wheel until the vehicle's door swung open, turning on the dome light.

And he saw Paige McKaslin emerging into the storm, dressed in a dark-green parka and brown hat, mittens and scarf. It was all he noticed because humiliation was starting to drag him down.

What on earth is *she* doing here? He lowered the shovel with great effort. Even moving his arms made his back spasm even more. Wind battered him. Falling snow pummeled him. But neither was as hard to endure as the woman's agile progress along the freshly shoveled pathway.

"Evan! I hope you don't mind I dropped by. I tried calling. I looked your number up before I left the diner, but there was no answer."

Be strong. Stoic. Cool. Although how he was going to do that and act as if he wasn't in agony remained a mystery. "I've been out shoveling the walk. About this time, I miss the boys. They were handy for chores like this."

"And I bet it was much easier on your back when they did the shoveling."

"Now, why would you say that? There's nothing wrong with me. I'm a man in the prime of my life. A little shoveling is nothing to me."

"Is that right? Then why do you look as if you're frozen in one position?"

"I'm a little cold, is all."

"And the grimace on your face is from seeing me?"

"Uh, not so much. I think my back went out. I have a bad disk."

"I thought I recognized that particular look of torture. Can you move?" Paige shifted the heavy sack she carried to her other arm and tracked up the icy concrete walkway. "Do you need help?"

"My pride has taken a serious blow today, but I think I'll live."

Paige tried not to be affected by the sight of him. With all his wide capable strength, he didn't appear decrepit. He somehow seemed even more masculine and powerful as he lowered the shovel to the ground and leaned on it like a cane. "What brings you by?"

"I owe you an apology." She lifted the sack, concentrating on it because she didn't want to look at him in case dislike for her showed on his face. "You surprised me so much, Evan, I just didn't realize what I was saying. I'm sorry."

"Don't worry about it." He looked like a pillar of steel. Strong. Unyielding. Unfeeling.

She'd never felt so awkward in her life. Maybe she'd been wrong. Maybe he'd hardly cared that she'd said no. So how foolish was it that she was standing here, fixing something that wasn't broken and now making everything worse?

She'd never been in this situation before. Her teenage years had not been average. She'd never dated; she had the responsibilities of her younger brother and sisters. She had grownup problems and no time to date. It wasn't until Jimmy had started working at the diner that she'd had her first real taste of romance. Felt the first flutter of joy at seeing that special man's face, hearing his voice, spending time just talking and getting to know him. Experienced the first wishes for sweet kisses and holding hands and hopes for a happy marriage.

Look how that turned out. She'd been so wrong then. She was probably just as wrong now. "At least let me leave this with you."

"That looks like a meal from the diner."

"It's more than that. It's not only a peace offering, but also a chicken dinner of appreciation. You keep insisting on paying for your meals instead of letting me give you a meal in thanks, so I'm bringing supper to you. Did you think I was a pushover? That I was a woman who gave up easily?"

Evan remained motionless. "I guess I never much thought about that."

Okay, I guess that's answer enough. She was making way too much of this. No wonder he was staring at her as though he was in the greatest pain. He was put out. She'd never been to his place before, although she drove past his driveway numerous times every day.

She'd never been much more than a distant acquaintance with him, despite the fact that they'd had teenage sons in sports and school and church groups together. He'd asked her to come to a Bible study with him, not exactly the full-blown date she was making this out to be. *What do you bet he's really regretting asking me to go with him now?*

It was time to fix what mess she'd made and retreat. "I hope you'll accept this in good faith. Are you still thinking about coming to this week's Bible study?"

"Couldn't say."

"I don't want you to miss out because of how I've behaved."

"That's not it. Really." Okay, that wasn't exactly the truth, Evan thought as he fought the blinding pain hacking through his spine, but it was close enough. Now he wasn't sure if he would go. What if his back was still out? At least he could salvage his pride. "It was nice of you to stop by. Are you working at the diner tonight?"

She looked flustered. And if it was possible for

Paige to look lovelier, then she certainly did now. A delicate pink bloomed across her cheeks and nose from the cold but also from her emotions as she glanced longingly in the direction of her vehicle. "I shouldn't have bothered you. I'll let you get back to your shoveling. Want me to put this on the step for you?"

Since he didn't want to admit he couldn't move, he nodded and made a grunt that would pass for a "yes." He gave thanks that he wasn't blocking the pathway to the porch because a herd of rampaging buffalo couldn't have forced him to move an inch out of the way.

Trying not to breathe too deeply and not to force his spine to move in the slightest, he prayed, *God, please let this pain end.* He wasn't sure if he was asking for relief from the physical or emotional agony.

He could tell Paige thought he was mad at her. That he was holding against her the fact that she'd turned him down. How did he admit that he had bigger problems, like the ability to stand tall the way a man should and not whimper? Stand tough, Thornton. It's only a little back pain.

Determined to maintain mind over matter, Evan tilted his head in her direction. The resulting strain on his lower spine wasn't too bad. Encouraging. Maybe he could fix this situation he'd found himself in with a few kind words. "That's mighty decent of you, Paige, to come all this way."

"It's all right. I owe you, too, for recommending Phil. He walked me through the first phase of repairs he wants to do, and I know he's given me an extremely low price. I suspect that might have something to do with you."

"I just told him how hard you work to keep that diner going and supporting your family is all. Phil's a family man. He knows what that takes. I'm glad you're happy with him. After all, your diner is where I eat most of my dinners these days."

"I wouldn't want that to change. Or for you to feel as if you couldn't risk coming in and seeing me behind the counter." She slipped the sack on the top step of the porch, and even in her layers of winter wear, she moved like poetry. Lithe and limber and graceful.

He felt it again, that overwhelming impulse gathering on his tongue. Just like before. He wanted to stop her from leaving. He wanted to ask her to stay, and he already knew her answer. She had a diner to run, she wasn't interested, she didn't date and she probably thought he was a dud for standing as still as a rock in his front yard. Somehow he managed to keep the words inside as she swept past, leaving a strange impression like a touch to his soul. He didn't breathe freely until she was safely buckled behind the wheel of her Jeep and backing up to turn around in the driveway.

As he watched her vehicle's taillights blink red in the gathering dusk, he felt the pain return in full force. The wintry wind sliced through him as if he were standing outside only in his drawers. He shivered, but it wasn't only the physical cold he felt. Or only physical pain.

*Why, God? Are you trying to tell me something?*

Maybe it was just loneliness, Evan reasoned, but that didn't explain that he'd never experienced this feeling around any other woman. No other had ever made him want to set aside the disaster Liz—and marriage—had brought him and try again. Because, he couldn't help thinking, loneliness was another kind of painful disaster in a man's life and maybe, with a different woman, a better woman, the outcome might be different, too.

He thought of what Phil had with his Marie. He thought of other people who seemed happy in their relationships. As Paige's Jeep pulled toward the last corner in the driveway, ready to disappear around a large stand of fir trees at the bend, he wondered if she ever wished for a different life and for someone to love, too.

Alone, in the quiet hours of the night, when no one could hear or know, and when the sting of loneliness seemed the greatest, did she, too, wish for a marriage that could work, for a happy connection to another? For that special kind of love you read about and saw in movies, a gentle, welcome place?

The shovel slipped from his fingers and thudded to the ground at his feet. Before he remembered his back, he automatically tried to bend to pick it up and then realized, as the vicious pain axed through his disk, that he couldn't move. Right. Only thinking about a woman could be powerful enough to make a man forget about a slipped disk.

Agony wrenched through his spine. He couldn't stand here forever, that was for sure, but he didn't seem able to move either. The Jeep's taillights disappeared from his peripheral vision and he was utterly alone.

The tap, tap of the falling snow, the whisper of the wind through the trees, the solemn feeling of a winter's cold settled around him.

Okay, he was tough. He could handle a little back pain. All it was going to take was a little willpower. And, he thought, a little prayer. With Herculean effort, he shuffled his boot an inch and shifted his weight. Since it was progress, he didn't complain.

Any second now his back was going to release, his spine was going to snap painfully back into place and he'd be able to get back in the house like the man he was, the man who worked out at the gym five days a week.

That second just hadn't happened yet. But he was a patient man. He dragged his left leg, enduring the pain traveling through his hip and down his thigh, and inched closer to the walkway.

That's when he heard the roar of an engine, muffled through the heavy curtain of snow. Maybe Paige was having problems with drifted snow on the driveway. He hoped she made it back to town safely. He thought about heading in her direction just to make sure she didn't need help, but then he realized that by the time he made it all the way down the mile-long driveway, it would be midnight. She was a competent woman; she seemed as if she could handle anything.

He liked that about her. He liked the idea of being with a woman who was strong enough to face life's hardships. He liked a lot of things about Paige Mc-Kaslin, and he didn't want to. A man ought at least to have control of who he liked and why, but in this one instance, it seemed out of his hands.

Suddenly, the wind changed and brought with it the alarming sense that he wasn't alone. He knew who was standing in the driveway behind him. He knew, because apparently he wasn't in control of this either, of how his and Paige's lives were currently intersecting.

"Having problems, there, tough guy?"

"I hope you're not mocking me. My dignity's taken enough blows as it is."

"You can stop pretending. I was so busy watching you in my rearview that I didn't watch where I was going. I'm caught in a drift. You could have plowed your driveway, you know."

"If I'd gotten out the tractor, then I wouldn't have thrown out my back."

"You never know. A big, muscle-bound man like you is bound to have one weakness."

She was next to him, grabbing hold of his arm. She was a tall woman, taller than he'd first thought, but he realized, her slenderness was deceptive. She might look willowy, but there was no mistaking the strength in her grip as she helped him take another step.

Too bad his brain wasn't working right, because all he could think was, She thinks I'm big and muscle-bound. He really shouldn't be glad about that, right?

"I have no weaknesses that I'll admit to."

That made her laugh, and it was a pleasant sound. Not brassy or fake, but low and pleasant like a kitten's purr. "That's just like a man. Never show your vulnerable side. I know. It's why my son drives me nuts."

"Is that the only reason?"

"No." She laughed again. "Can you get up the stairs, or will I have to carry you?"

"I'd like to see you try." He weighed two hundred pounds. She couldn't be more than one twenty-five. "There's no sense putting your back out, too."

"My lumbar disks thank you."

"You have a bad back, too?"

"I like to blame it on carrying heavy trays of food for about two decades, but since I don't like to admit I'm over thirty-five, I can't use it as an excuse."

"You don't need the excuse, Paige. You don't look a day older than thirty."

"Careful. We'll be lucky if a bolt of lightning doesn't streak from the sky and strike us where we stand."

"No lightning, see?" He dragged his foot onto the bottom step, refusing to lean on Paige because he was no weakling, and did his best not to let on that the pain was killing him. "I wasn't lying. You're an amazing woman. You're lovely and you know how to cook some of the best—"

Lightning seared through the storm, arrowing like a bright finger from heaven to the trees behind the house. There was an explosion of thunder above and the crack of a pine tree beyond, and then there was utter silence.

Paige started to laugh. "I can't believe it. Lightning struck."

"Now don't go taking this the wrong way, Paige. You might think I wasn't telling the truth, but I was.

Why else would I have asked you out? I haven't done that since I was in college. I told you that."

What was it about this man's low rumbling voice that seemed to knock all common sense right out of her? Paige wanted to believe him, she really did, because she hated to admit it, but Evan Thornton—the *man* and not the customer—was starting to grow on her.

He could make her laugh, and she'd never appreciated the importance of a sense of humor in a man before. Tiny laugh lines crinkled around his handsome eyes, and it had a devastating effect.

Not that she could let it affect her. He was handsome, he was distinguished, and he was no thrill-seeking teenager. Not this man who'd built this fine house and made it a secure home for his young boys to have grown up in.

It took a lot of character to be the parent that stayed. A lot of strength to handle the hard—although rewarding—parts of being a father. And this man looked as if he could weather anything with good humor to boot—even the back pain that he was too proud to let her see full-force.

She knelt to snatch up the diner's sack and propped open the storm door, since the handle was on her side. But Evan was taking none of that. Apparently no woman helped him. He seemed to be all male pride and ego as he grabbed the door and held it for her, even though his face went white from the strain.

"I hope you don't mind if I use your phone. My cell isn't working with this storm." She stepped into the warmth, grateful for it, but not expecting the rush of tenderness for the stubborn, strong, un-yielding man who limped in after her.

Men. She'd forgotten there was a lot of good in them, too. And wasn't that the danger?

## Chapter Seven

Evan craned his back the few necessary inches so he could reach the door and shut it against the shower of snow. Pain exploded once again in his lower back and, with the scrape of bone against his disk, his back was relatively back in place. Residual pain shivered through his left leg, but he gave a prayer of thanks heavenward.

"Oh, that was your back?" Paige must have heard the popping sound. Her rosebud mouth had softened into a concerned O, and sympathy shadowed her deep-blue eyes. "Evan, you need to get some ice on that. Do you have some anti-inflammatories?"

He couldn't answer. He could only stare at her as she set down her sack and her purse and untied her coat's hood. Coming closer as if naturally meaning to help out. He'd been facing problems—even something as minor as a strained back—alone for so long, he couldn't seem to wrap his mind around it. She was coming at him and in the half-light of the foyer she looked mysterious, cloaked in shadow, but also warm and vibrant with life, her heart showing vulnerable and open.

"You've got to give that some rest. Let's get you into the living room. Is it this way?" Again she took his arm, but he couldn't stand to let her think he was weak. He intended to shake his arm away from the warm, firm grip she had, but he couldn't stand that idea either. "I'm all right. It's been a while since you've been around a wounded man, right?"

"Oh, you don't want my help. Fine. Limp into the living room all on your own steam and I'll get some ice for you. Unless you're too stubborn to let me do that for you?"

"You think I'm amusing. I can tell. Your eyes are sparkling."

"The male gender can be very amusing. Sometimes." She released him, trouble quirking her soft mouth into a sweet smile. "Or maybe I just like to see a man suffering. It's appropriate."

"Hey, I'm one of the good guys."

"I didn't say you weren't." She left him to his own maneuvering.

Good thing. He didn't think he could keep pretending everything was all right. He limped over to the sectional in the living room. The crackling fire sent warm soothing radiant heat over him. He was frozen clear through, but that seemed the least of his worries.

His back was aching like a cracked tooth, and he sighed with relief as he eased onto the cushions. The fire's warmth enveloped him like an electric blanket. The tension in his back eased up a bit. Much better.

"Here's an ice pack." She bustled through the house with the same snappy efficiency that she used in the diner. "I've got two anti-inflammatories, a glass of water. If you want, I can heat up the dinner I brought over while I wait for the tow truck. Sound good?"

"Paige, you're not on duty here. This is my home. You don't need to wait on me."

"I don't mind." She handed him a sealed plastic bag of ice, wrapped in a kitchen towel, and set the glass and ibuprofen caplets on a saucer on the coffee table. "I'll be right back."

Why would any man leave her, he wondered, not because she was fetching him what he needed, but because she was so caring about it. It was easy for him to see the real Paige, the woman with a big heart she seemed to be afraid to show to the general public. She was a private person, he realized. Was she, he wondered, as lonely in her life as he was?

He popped the pills and washed them down with

a swallow of water. As he positioned the lumpy ice pack against the small of his back, he could hear her in the kitchen. The whisper of cabinet doors opening. The clink of plates and the rustle of the big paper sack.

It had been a strange sensation to see a woman in his house bustling around and taking care of things. Fortunately it didn't bring back memories of Liz, because she'd never been the efficient, get-things-done type.

What it made him think of was, not the past, but the present. How good it was to hear the movements of another person in this way-too-big house. How comforting it was to hear the gentle pad of a woman's footsteps and gentle voice in the other room.

Yearning filled him. It was a sweet and rich longing, and more powerful than he'd ever known before. A longing for what he didn't really believe in. And yet it felt right there within his reach. Being with a woman—a wife—in a way that was compatible and companionable, but it was more than that. Not just love of the heart but of something deeper.

And exactly why was he thinking this way? His back must be hurting worse than he thought, to make him so sentimental.

"Bad news." She returned with a plate full of dinner salad glistening with Italian dressing. "The tow truck isn't going to be here any time soon. I'd be better off hoofing it back to town."

"I could take you."

"My rig's blocking your driveway." She slipped the plate and the paper napkin and fork onto the coffee table in front of him. "I've got a call in to Alex. He can finish up his dinner at the church and come rescue me."

"I think I can handle freeing up your Jeep. I've got a winch on my truck. It'll be no problem."

"And what about your back?"

"It's fine. Just a little stitch, that's all."

"Sure it is, tough guy." Paige wasn't fooled one bit. "What is it with you men? You can't show an ounce of weakness?"

"Exactly. Never let your guard down. I bet you know something about that."

"Okay, now you're getting too personal." She wasn't sure what to do with Evan Thornton. He sat there with his hair tousled, looking about as rugged and welcome as a dream man, but he was real and sincere. She liked him. She didn't want to, but she did. "I don't want my reputation as an ice queen ruined. It's kept all those bothersome suitors away for years."

"Why would you want that? You like being alone?"

His question surprised her like a right hook and her knees wobbled. She sank to the couch, not at all sure what to say with her heart jack-hammering in her chest, and Evan's gaze unwavering. It felt as if he saw too much of her, and she wasn't sure how to stop him. "Now you are being way, way too personal."

"I guess you're like me. Alone is better than betrayal."

Like an ax hitting her chest, her heart cracked wide open. Sometimes it felt as if she were the only person on earth who'd had a disappointing marriage at best, and a devastating wound she'd shown no one. Ever. "In the diner, it's like all I see are couples. Married people are everywhere. Young and old and in between. With kids, without kids and empty-nesters. It's not the happy couples I notice. It's the ones that sit in silence. They don't talk. They don't look at one another. And I think how lucky I am not to be with someone who sees past me."

"My wife saw me just fine. She just wasn't content with what she saw."

"How could that be? All anyone needs to know about you is to see what a fine job you did raising your sons."

*I could kiss you, lady.* Evan's chest cinched tight. Her compliment surprised him, but it did more than that. It touched him where he was vulnerable, in the deepest places of his heart. He'd tried so hard for his boys' sake. It hadn't always been easy, especially not alone, but then Paige would understand that. She would know how it felt to be alone raising kids. "That means a lot coming from someone who's raised a good kid, too."

"He is a good kid, but I keep my eye on him. I'll get your supper in the microwave and you should be set. Is there anything else you need?"

"Paige, I'm serious. Don't wait on me." He stood, refusing to acknowledge the grimace of pain in his back or the residual traveling pain making its presence known in his leg. "I think whatever popped out of place has popped back. Let me grab my keys and I'll help you out of the drift."

"You shouldn't be up moving around."

"Hey, I'm tough. That's the first lesson you've got to know about me. Not much can get me down, and if it does, it doesn't keep me there."

"Note taken. I'll never try to suggest you take it easy again."

"Excellent." Evan couldn't say why her smile lit him up inside, but the effect was like a ray of light on the dark side of the moon as he limped over to get his keys.

The storm had worsened since she'd been in Evan's house. She shivered, swiped the wind-driven snow from her eyes and tried to see him in the near whiteout conditions. The stubborn man just didn't know when to stop.

Or maybe it was just her perspective. She hadn't been around a man in a personal capacity in a long, long time, excluding her son, who was more boy than adult at this point of his life.

Evan Thornton had to be in agony, she knew because she had a slipped disk that bothered her from time to time, so she knew what it felt like. And he was acting as if he was impervious to pain, as if he hadn't just been unable to move less than twenty-five minutes ago.

He straightened from the winch on the front of his rig, highlighted by the headlights that cast him in silhouette. Invincible, he seemed to rise up to his six-foot height and from her vantage on the down slope of the hillside, he seemed ten feet tall.

In that moment, her breath caught between her ribs and she couldn't explain what happened within her; she only knew that something in her heart felt different simply from looking at him. He cut through the beams of light and blended with the night. Although her eyes could not make him out against the dark and the storm, it was as if her heart could sense him standing there, unbowed and mighty, like some Wild-West hero brought to life.

She didn't believe in heroes. Not at all. Not in real

life. Not in her experience. So why was she thinking this way? Was it simply the possibility of the fairy tale of true love worming its way into her thoughts again, after all this time and all her experience to the contrary? She'd banished the hope long ago when Jimmy had walked away from the grill and out the door with a fun, young blond thing while she'd had a crying baby with an earache, a busy diner and a call from the deputy about her younger sister in hot water again.

A woman had to stand on her own two feet in this tough world. She shouldn't be wasting her energy wishing for a white knight on a shining stallion to rescue her from her problems. The only help she needed was God's help.

The driving wind chose that moment to ram against her so hard, she lost her balance, tumbling against the snow-driven door of her Jeep. Visibility vanished and she lost sight of the mythical man she'd woven out of old daydreams. Out of loneliness, too, she had to admit. For the business of her days and the fullness of her life, she was alone in the most fundamental way.

Maybe that's just the way life was, she'd been even lonelier when she'd been married all those years ago. She'd felt so utterly lonely, wanting the loving tenderness from her husband who would rather watch football or play his video games or go out playing pool with his buddies.

This loneliness was better, she told herself firmly, cloaked and isolated by the drifting snow and pummeled by a wildly vicious wind, she did the only thing she could. Called out a thank you to Evan, wherever he was—if he had any sense, he'd be in the warm cab of his truck right now—and she fought the gusts to open her vehicle's door, where the idling engine was blowing hot blasts from the vents—but the temperature outside was so cold, it did little to warm the interior of the Jeep.

With her teeth chattering from the frigid conditions, she hopped onto the seat and slammed the door.

And gave a jump when the passenger door opened and a dark presence slid into the other seat. The wind slammed the door shut and they sat in the glow of the dome light, the gusts shaking the vehicle and howling wildly around them.

"I can see why the drifts got so deep." Evan's low baritone rumbled as warm as firelight.

"I'm going to have a fine time getting back to town. I'd best get going. I owe you—again—for helping me."

"Then I expect you to pay up." His words were softened by a mysterious crick of his mouth in a sly—and very charming lopsided grin—as he flicked on her radio and hit the scanning button. "Thought you might want to hear this."

She already knew with a punch of certainty which channel he was scanning for—one of the local stations, which was in the middle of an emergency broadcast. All county roads were closed due to extremely dangerous weather conditions. "I left the twins in charge of the diner."

"Then call them and tell them to close up. They live right there in town, right?"

She nodded. The journey home for them would be relatively safe. "I can ask Dave to drive them on his way. He's an old hand at dealing with this weather."

"Then did you want to come back with me and use my phone?"

"No, I'd better risk getting home. Although, I'm not that sure how long that's going to take me. Could I ask you another favor?"

"Try me."

It went against her grain to ask anyone for help like this, but she thought of the girls' safety—there wasn't anything more important than that. "Could you call the diner for me?"

"Consider it done. You'd best get going before this gets any worse, and we both know it can. Be safe." He opened the door to the fury of the blizzard conditions. "You're going to owe me big-time. How about escorting me on Wednesday night? You'd be doing me a favor. I'm shy."

"You're not shy."

"No, but help me out here. Go with the flow, like my boys say. It's a new meeting. I'm afraid to go alone."

"A big strong man like you? You don't seem afraid of anything."

"I'm big on the outside, marshmallow on the inside."

This man was *so* not fooling her. "No man is marshmallow on the inside."

"How do you know that? Are you an expert?" A quirk of humor tugged at the corner of his mouth.

Yeah, he was charming, all right. What was a girl to do? "Let's just say I have had practical experience with the species."

"Well, some men fall outside the normal bell curve of averages. That would be me."

"So, you're below average?"

That made his dark eyes twinkle. "I was thinking more of the other side of the chart. More than your average guy."

"I'm not sure that's a good thing."

"Then it's a date?"

"No. I'm not agreeing to a date. I don't date."

"Neither do I. Then how about one Bible studier helping out a wannabe Bible studier."

"Haven't we been here before? Why would my answer be different?"

"Well, you've had time to think about it. You've had time to see I'm an okay guy—I mean, above average. I at least come with morals, principles and good references."

If she wasn't careful, she was going to start liking him even more. "Okay. Agreed. I'll go to the coffee house with you, but it's not a date."

"Not a date. Two people just going to a Bible study together. Good night, Paige." He shut the door and he was gone. Not even the faintest hint of him remained as the fierce storm closed in around her, leaving her alone again. *Alone,* being the key word.

What was it about Evan Thornton that made her feel the sting of loneliness when he was gone? She hated to think about it. She didn't want to admit she had any shred of that young, foolish girl she'd once been left inside her. She was a practical, hard-working woman who knew how to get things done. What was it that she heard endlessly from people? Sensible to a fault. Yep, that was her. So why on earth was she wishing that she'd said yes to Evan as a date instead of as a friend?

Because I'm insane. It was the only thing that made sense. Maybe it was some sort of mid-life crisis. Or a reaction to all the long backbreaking hours she'd been working. A woman couldn't put in horribly long work days seven days a week forever. Something was bound to give…apparently, today, it was her sanity.

I'd better schedule an afternoon off and soon.

Well…she amended. Maybe after the month's financial statements were done. As she sat forward, as if that would help her see better through the snow battering the windshield, she realized that while she was heading home, it would be no night of leisure. There was the bookwork to do. At least she had all but the day's receipts at home. She'd do a little computer work until bedtime.

Even in four-wheel drive, the tires caught and spun in the deep drifts that covered the driveway like waves in an ocean.

Driving kept her full attention, and it was a fortunate thing she had her full attention to give. Surely the youth pastor had sent the kids home before the emergency bulletin came through. She prayed that Alex was home safe.

But it wasn't worry over her son that troubled her as she battled to keep the Jeep on the road. No, for some reason she couldn't explain, the soreness of being alone remained, as if the memory of Evan's impressive presence remained like a ghost to haunt her.

*You're going to owe me big-time,* he'd said, as though it was a threat. What on earth did he mean? She'd accompany him to Bible study, introduce him so he wasn't alone, and they'd be square, right? That's what he meant, right?

The uncertainty stayed with her on the arduous half-mile journey to the private road that took her to her own driveway. To her relief Alex's truck was parked squarely in the middle of the drive, caught in a drift, and so she parked behind him, knowing there was no way to get around.

The wind struck her like a boxer's fists, and she couldn't remember feeling a colder one, ever. The night and the darkness felt endlessly isolating as she fought her way through the drifts, and along her driveway cut between snowbound pines. The wind moaned through the snow-heavy limbs overhead, and she hurried as fast as she could manage through the blizzard conditions and to the house that emerged from the whiteout, lit windows glowing gold. There was Alex in the open doorway, calling out, glad to see her.

Not so lonesome anymore, she hurried out of the storm, hugged her son even though he protested, and gave thanks that they were safe and snug as the late-season blizzard raged on.

It was nearly an hour later by the time Evan shoveled the drifts out of the way so the garage door could close properly. He'd done as Paige had asked, returned to call the diner, given the evening cook her message and banked the fire so he could go right back out in the storm.

And why? He was frozen half to death in the sub-zero temperatures and even colder windchill, and his back hurt so bad he couldn't straighten up all the way. . .and all for a woman. A woman who made him half crazy, judging by the way he was acting.

Although the roads were beyond dangerous to drive in, what had he done? He'd followed the wheel tracks Paige's Jeep had left in the snow all the way to her driveway. Just to make sure she wasn't lost in the ditch somewhere.

When he'd come across her vehicle parked neatly in the dark behind her son's truck, unable to go any farther, he knew she must be home safe, since the walk wasn't far. Sure enough the message light blinked on the answering machine. Since he was half-stooped anyway, he didn't have much of a reach to hit Play.

"Hey Evan, I'm home safe. I hope you made it back up your driveway okay. Stay warm and take care of your back. Take another ibuprofen, okay?"

Was it his imagination, or was there more than friendly warmth in Paige's voice? The machine beeped and whirred to a stop.

Agony ripped through his spine as he marched over to the fireplace, stirred the coals and added kindling to the glowing red chunks. The cedar kindling caught instantly and flame licked through the thin slivers of wood.

He crumpled paper, trying to drown out the sound and the memory of Paige's voice and of her presence here in his house, in his home, making the loneliness so strident, it was a physical pain he could not deny.

*What are you trying to tell me, Lord?* he asked as he tossed split wood into the fire. There came no answer, although the howling winds and scouring snow against the siding and along the eaves echoed in the stillness surrounding him.

He stretched for the remote and turned on the TV just for the noise. Just to make the emptiness less dark and less shadowed.

# Chapter Eight

*Tonight's the night.* It was all Paige had thought about for the last hour of her shift, and it was all she could think about now as she capped the tall chocolate-banana milkshake. The diner was quieting down, and she was keeping one eye on the door waiting for Evan Thornton to walk through it.

"Ain't it about time for you to leave?" Dave commented through the order-up window as he finished up a burger on the grill. "I've got things covered."

"Thanks. If things get busy, and you need backup, I've got my cell. You call, I'll come."

"You seem awful eager. Thought you liked that Bible study you go to."

Was that a smirk she saw beneath his mustache? Just how much did he know? She hadn't told a soul about her arrangement with Evan. After all, they were acquaintances. That was it. She was doing him a favor, because he'd done her a favor. Right?

And if thinking of Evan made her feel a little lighter, then she didn't have to have a reason for it, did she? It wasn't as if anything serious was going to come of this. She'd meet him. Take him to Bible study. Introduce him. End of story. It was no big deal.

"I'm always eager to go, you know that." She kept going on her way through the dining room. Brianna looked as though she had everything under control. She gave the teenager a smile as they passed in the aisle.

"I didn't get even one overring all shift!" The teenager beamed. "Can you believe it?"

"Absolutely. You're good, girl."

"Yeah!" She practically skipped to the front.

Well, that's progress. Paige could only hope Brandilyn's mastery of the cash register wasn't far behind. She slid the milkshake cup onto Alex's table, careful of the papers scattered over the surface.

His physics book was open, and his blond head was bent over his current problem. Lost in concentration, he scribbled madly with his mechanical pencil.

She pulled a wrapped straw from her apron pocket and slipped it next to the large cup.

"Thanks, Mom." Alex scribbled down a final

number before he looked up. A deep frown of concentration dug into his forehead. "Whew. I think I nailed that. I've got one more."

"Then are you heading home?"

"You know it. Want me to check on Annie?"

The mare had figured out the latest latch on her stall door. "I'd appreciate it. Call if you need me."

"I know, Mom." He flashed her a charming grin. "You have a good time with Mr. Thornton."

"How did you know about that?"

"Little potatoes have big ears," he replied, something she always used to say when he was little. Proud of himself, he grabbed the straw and tore off the wrapper. "You left it written down in your engagement diary. The one you leave open every day on the kitchen counter. It was hard to miss."

She'd never had anything really private to write in it before. "I'm gonna ground you for that."

"Empty threat." He grinned even more widely, sure of himself. If nothing, her son was confident and steady. He was going to make a fine man one day, and that made her proud.

And sad. She had so little time left with her son. She wanted to hold so tightly to him and never let go. But that wasn't good for him.

So, instead of grabbing him close, she settled for ruffling her fingertips through his hair, the way she'd done since he was a little guy. "I don't want you to get all worried. Mr. Thornton is coming to our Bible study for the first time and I told him I'd introduce him around."

"It's not a date?" He looked crestfallen.

"No. You know me. I'm too busy keeping up with you and this place to find time to date. Do you need anything else before I go?"

"Mom, dating might be good for you. You know, to round out your life."

"I wasn't aware my life needed rounding out."

"Sure. I saw it on *Dr. Phil.* You don't have enough balance." He flashed her "The Eye," as if he had the power to charm her into seeing things his way. "And Pastor John said that you're going to have a hard time when I go, with the empty-nest thing, so I have to be understanding. So I'm being understanding. Go. Date. I want to support you in your life choices."

Yeah, he thought he was so funny with that glint in his eye, so confident and young. "Those are my lines, and I—"

The bell over the door chimed, announcing a new customer. Why did she automatically spin to see if it was Evan walking through her door?

"He's here." Alex waggled his brows. "And he brought flowers. Yeah, this is *so* not a date."

"He just has good manners."

"Sure, Mom, whatever you say." Alex gave her a knowing look as he took a long pull on his milkshake. Like any teenager, he thought he knew everything.

And he would be wrong. Evan wasn't interested in her. How could he be? Like her, he was probably work-weary and, since he'd never remarried, he probably liked it that way. She understood about wounds that no one could see, and they had a profound influence on the way someone lived their life.

"Paige." Evan held out the wrapped bouquet of yellow tulips and daisies, small and modest and friendly. "I noticed you always keep fresh flowers by the cash register, so when I saw these I thought you could use them."

See? Good manners, just as she'd thought. "They're lovely, and that's thoughtful of you, considering I'm the one who owes you a favor."

"After tonight, we're even." He handed her the flowers with a good-humored grin.

"Unless something else comes up and you help me out again." She brushed the edge of a daisy's silken petals with her fingertips. "Brianna, could you put these in water? And you can handle things until I get back?"

"Yeah, and Dave's, like, in charge. So chill and have a good time with Mr. Thornton." Brianna cracked her gum and waggled her brows.

It was probably hard for a teenage girl to understand. Paige knew, because she'd once been like that, too, filled with ideas of romance. But no more. She fetched her book bag from beneath the front counter and grabbed her jacket from the rack by the door. It surprised her when Evan caught hold of the sleeve and helped her into her coat.

He was only being a gentleman, which he proved again as he held the door for her. She listened to the delighted goodbyes from Alex and Brianna and rolled her eyes.

"At least it's a nice enough evening that we can walk."

"It is." Was that his attempt at starting a conversation? Paige listened to the echo of their shoes on the concrete. "It looks as if your back is doing better."

"I'm happy to say I made a full recovery."

"Now that there's no snow to shovel?"

"Yep. I want you to know I'm fit and hearty, and that was only a momentary weakness."

"I never doubted your vitality. You're just past forty."

He laughed. "Thanks. I feel so much better now."

"Glad I could help." She liked the way small, hardly noticeable character lines cut into the corners of his eyes. He really was a handsome man, she thought, in a *friendly* way. "I want to thank you again for recommending Phil. I've hired him to start renovations."

"Sounds like that leak was just the start of your problems."

"It's sad but true. Phil's promised that he can keep me open for business through just about everything. The customers won't even know he's there."

"Good. A lot of folks depend on your diner."

"I know. Some days it's just nice not to have to cook. I'm thankful that so many people come to my place when they're feeling like that."

"Are you kidding? You've got some of the best food in the county. Why do you think I drive all the way from work, and past I don't know how many restaurants on the way, for your roasted chicken and dumplings? So, what do you do when you're too tired to cook?"

"That's not a luxury I have, but I don't mind."

They waited for a lone minivan to amble along the street. Paige recognized her cousin Karen behind the wheel, as she slowed to wave and smile. It didn't take a psychic to figure out what her cousin was thinking. Evan was standing at her side, with less than a few inches between them.

Anyone watching would leap to the wrong conclusion. It was strange, because the male at her side was usually her son. Now, she was walking through town with a handsome, eligible bachelor.

Paige waved as Karen drove by. As she and Evan stepped off the curb in sync, she gathered her courage. It might be her only time to ask such a personal question. "How did you manage after your youngest son went off to college?"

He missed a step but recovered his balance. "That's a tough question."

"Sorry. It's probably too personal. I didn't mean—"

"No, it's all right." He quickly reassured her, jamming his hands into his jacket pockets. "I could say something easy, like I finally had some peace and quiet."

"That's overrated."

"It is. I now have sole possession of the remote control. No teenager making messes in my kitchen, my bathroom or my car."

"Apparent plusses."

"On the surface, yeah. I also don't have to sit up waiting for Cal to come in at night, trying not to worry about every disaster that could happen on the road between the Youth Center in town and home. But it's not the real truth. Not at all."

Paige heard the hitch of emotion in his rumbling baritone. She wondered at the depth of feeling that lay hidden beneath the surface. "I bet your house seems empty. I know my home sure will be."

And because that hurt, she stared down at the blacktop beneath her sneakers and tried to swallow past her tight throat. It wasn't just her house that would be empty, but her life.

"The truth is, I can't get over missing them. I'm glad for my boys. They both have good starts in this world. They are smart and strong and make solid decisions. I did everything I could to raise them up to be good men. I've never been so proud."

"You did a good job."

"At the same time, I've lost my sons. They will never again be my boys running through my house, making enough noise to drive a normal person crazy."

She liked that he smiled, and dimples dug into his lean cheeks. She could just bet he was a wonderful father. She could feel all he did not say. "They're men, now."

"Yep. It's the way it's meant to be, but the void they leave behind is something that can suck you down like light in a black hole, if you let it."

"That's what I'm afraid of. I've taken care of everyone for most of my life. I raised my brother and sisters and my Alex. I used to think that I missed my chance at my own life. I went from being a child to an orphan and right into being a responsible adult. I don't regret it."

"Neither do I. Not for a second."

Paige had to like him better for his words. "I always figured when my son was raised, I would finally get my chance to do what I want. Now that that time is here, it's not exciting at all. I don't want things to change."

"It's bittersweet."

"Exactly."

Evan slowed as the sidewalk on the other side of the street neared. "Running the diner isn't what you want?"

"It was never my life's ambition, but it has kept me busy and my family provided for."

"It's a pretty integral part of this town. Folks drive for miles just for your chocolate milkshakes."

"So people tell me." She left their conversation at that, stepping up her pace until she was on the sidewalk, getting a little ahead of him.

Some things hurt too much. Her future should be an exciting one; it was a new phase of life for her, too. It was scary to think about, but she wanted to go to college. Maybe travel a bit. But the fun things she'd always planned on doing one day did not look as exciting now as they'd been before.

The night felt colder and the dark oppressive, and she could not escape into the light and warmth fast enough, away from the hurt she knew was to come. Alex wasn't just her son. He was her whole life. And now that her sisters had married and their lives were so busy, Alex was all she had left.

After he moved away, she would be alone. Truly alone. For the first time in her life.

Evan sat at one of the small wooden tables in the town's coffee shop, unable to purge Paige's words from his mind. *Now that that time is here, it's not exciting at all. I don't want things to change.*

Change was inevitable. That was simply life. He knew that from first-hand experience. The major turning points in his life had never been of his choosing. When he looked back, it wasn't his logical thoughts that had chosen Liz for a wife. His heart had. A pure leap of faith and heart. They had been happy for a little while.

But her betrayal had been out of his control. Time passed and as the boys grew up and left home. The decades of his life seemed to be adding up. And, he feared, he was all out of turning points. All out of new directions. He wanted his life to change. He wasn't happy.

After hearing Paige's words tonight, he knew he wasn't alone. *So, Lord, what does that mean?*

He didn't expect the good Father to answer. As Karen Drake, part owner of the shop and cousin to Paige, spoke about the changes in her life, he stared at his own Bible. The black type blurred against the crisp white page.

*Lord, what do You have in store for me, which will bring me hope and a good future?*

He wanted his life to change. He'd lived for his sons. For many, many years that had been more than enough. But the endless months of solitude had become a sadness that he feared would go on forever.

He feared that the long loneliness of his future would be broken up by the occasional phone call from the boys, and, as time passed, they would come with their wives and children to visit. But when they left, the loneliness would be sharper. The sadness deeper.

The stages of life were inevitable. He could see that. The women who were wives and mothers, like Karen, managed to squeeze this Bible study into their busy schedules. One day those mothers would be where he was and Paige would soon be. Time was a relentless wheel always turning and leaving only memories behind.

He did not want to look back in one year or five or ten and see no real memories.

He didn't want to find that his heart had atrophied from having no one to love.

He did not know what the answer was. He didn't know if he could trust another woman enough to date again. He'd have to open his heart, open his life and hope that he wasn't on a path as destructive as his marriage had been.

As he looked around the room, he saw several settled couples. Husbands and wives who were raising their kids and had it together. They sat side by side, leaning slightly toward one another as if they were always just a little connected, even in public. Those secret looks, knowing smiles and silent communication spoke of the kind of bond Evan had never been privileged to know.

The hard punch of emotion in his chest, feelings he couldn't begin to sort out, left him distracted. He should be paying attention. But the lines before him seemed to brighten. Was it time to make a change?

The truth was, he'd learned the hard way that a marriage depended on both husband and wife working together. Making good choices. Renewing their love and commitment and belief in one another every day. Day by day. That was putting a whole lot of faith in another person.

What no one told you about marriage was that a man wasn't only putting his faith in the hope that love would last, but also in the woman he married. He had to have faith that every decision she would make in the years to come would be for the good.

When a man trusted a woman enough to marry her, he was trusting her with his heart, his soul, his children, his home, his finances, his everything. He'd been burned—and burned hard—by Liz.

But that didn't mean there weren't women who would never harm their husbands. Who would never hurt them. Never lie or cheat or betray the man they loved.

Why was he so aware of Paige at his side? Her presence shone through him like the warm rays of a summer sun and he felt illuminated.

Time flew. Before he knew it, he was muttering "Amen" following the final prayer. The small group was breaking up, talking and starting on their good-byes.

It surprised him how fast Paige had popped out of her chair and was busily stuffing her book and Bible into her big floral bag. She'd purposefully turned her back to him and was chatting with one of her cousins. Evan recognized the young lady. She was one of the younger girls in the family, and she'd worked at the diner during her teenage years. Kelly, he thought the girl's name was, gazed up at Paige with unmistakable admiration.

That's when it hit him once again the kind of lady Paige McKaslin really was. She gave away cinnamon rolls and connection. She worked endlessly to cook and serve other people. Her diner supported her family and many of her cousins through their school and college years. Her business was a place in the community where friends joined, and lonely souls could find a hot cup of good coffee and kindness.

No man is an island, he knew, and he didn't want to be alone anymore.

He hadn't believed he could find a woman he could trust. A woman who stayed, who faced her responsibilities, and who did so without bitterness and resentment.

How long had he prayed for such a woman to

love, to be a helpmate, just to have and to hold, after Liz had left and before the hurt she'd caused settled deep into his heart?

Forever. He'd given up. He'd let bitterness in. He'd closed off his heart to the possibility of ever being hurt like that again. And God's answer might have been in front of him all along.

## Chapter Nine

Sunday morning's torrential rain chased her through the diner's back door. What had happened to May's gentle weather? Where was spring?

The last few days had felt like total chaos, and with the morning sermon still fresh in her mind, Paige slipped her Bible on the end of the counter, shrugged out of her drenched raincoat, and vowed to put order back into her life.

No more stray thoughts about Evan Thornton. No more faint wishes for fairy tales. God had given her a perfectly good life; it was enough. In fact, it was more than enough. It took all her energy to keep it in order.

Look at the kitchen. She had slipped out to the early morning service, and see what happened in her absence. Prep work was scattered everywhere. "Alex!"

Where was that boy? And, with a sting of excitement, she wondered, where was Amy? Hadn't she turned up for work this morning? Had she been able to take a pregnancy test? Was she pregnant?

Joy at that happy thought chased away her annoyance at her wayward son. He was only a teenager, and therefore innately distractible, and so she'd simply hunt him down and get him back on task.

The bulk of their Sunday-morning business wouldn't hit until after the main morning service at the town churches, and so there was plenty of time to right this sinking ship.

"Alex?" She ignored the rainwater sluicing off the jacket as she hung it up. And, speaking of teenagers, where were the twins?

She wove through the abandoned kitchen and peeked out into the dining room—there were only the old-timers finishing up a quiet breakfast before heading over to services. Their cups looked freshly refilled and their plates had been bussed, so the twins couldn't have gone too far.

"Have you seen the kids?" she asked Ed Brisbane when she caught his eye.

"Don't know what they were up to. They were in the office arguing in whispers, but we could hear 'em."

"The office?" That didn't make any sense. She was the only one who handled the paperwork.

"Then I heard the back door slam shut. Haven't seen 'em since."

That can't be good. "Okay. Thanks. How about Amy?"

"Caught sight of her running down the hall looking like a woman with morning sickness." Ed's merry eyes twinkled. "At least, that's the way it looked to me."

"Me, too." Since the restrooms were closer, Paige hurried down the short hallway and burst through the door to find the twins hovering over the sinks.

"Paige! Amy's really, really sick!" They both flew at her, talking in unison.

It was a relief to see them; at least they weren't outside in this rain, for whatever reason. "Amy, are you all right?"

"Yes," came a weak reply from inside one of the stalls.

Definitely morning sickness, Paige thought as she rounded on the twins. "Where's Alex?"

"Uh…" Brianna traded worried glances with her twin.

Both girls said nothing more for a moment, as if stumped as to what to say. "He's, uh…"

*"Where is he?"* Alarm pounded through her. His truck had been parked in the back lot. He wouldn't have gone out on foot in this weather, right? "He's supposed to be helping with the brunch prep."

"I don't wanna tell ya." Brandilyn gave a longing look toward the door. "'Cuz it'll really upset ya and stuff."

Alarm transformed into panic. A thousand possible disasters zoomed into her mind. *"What is going on?* Just tell me."

"He's. . .he's on the r-roof," Brianna stammered. "It's, like, leaking."

"What?" All she could see was disaster. It was raining so hard. "You mean he's up on the roof? *Right now?"*

"Don't worry—"

"—but we've got a bucket under the leak—" the twins said in unison.

Amy's voice sounded, thin but steadfast, on the other side of the stall. "Paige, go after him. I didn't know—" And that's as far as she got.

"What do we do?" the twins asked breathlessly.

"Brandilyn, go hold her hair if you don't mind. Brianna, call Heath, ok? Amy, I'll be right back, sweetie."

There was only a moan of misery. Sympathy for her sister's condition fueled Paige's trek through the kitchen and out the back door. She, too, had been enormously sick the entire time she was carrying Alex. Making a mental note to take Amy off the schedule in no uncertain terms—allowing her light duty only when she was feeling well enough—she slipped back into her dripping raincoat and hurried out into what felt like a hurricane.

"Alex?" The deafening hammer of the rain drowned out the sound of her voice, even when she cupped her hands like a megaphone and tried again. Since there was no sign of him from where she stood, she circled around the side of the building. There wasn't a ladder on the premises, so that meant he'd had to climb onto the roof from the vacant upstairs apartment.

Sure enough, as she climbed the outside stairs to the apartment door, she caught sight of a flash of navy blue against the peak of the front side of the roof—she couldn't have spotted him when she pulled in. If she had, he'd be safe in the diner by now.

"Alex!" Rainwater cascaded down the asphalt shingles like a river at flood stage, and it had to make the roof impossibly slick. How exactly had he gotten up on that roof? "Alex!"

The storm was too loud for him to hear her. She could just make out the curve of his back, so she waved her arms, hoping to catch his attention. Nothing. She wasn't about to let him stay out here. The rain was bitter cold. He'd catch pneumonia if he wasn't careful, that is, if he didn't fall off the roof first.

Regretting that she hadn't had time for her usual morning yoga in the last six months, she felt her back groan as she climbed over the handrail and wedged the toes of her walking boots onto the lowest corner of the eave. Water raced in a torrent around her feet as she lunged forward and wrapped her arm around the rain gutter downspout, while icy water pounded down on her head and back.

Trying not to imagine the hard blacktopped ground two stories below, she clung to the downspout, which she seriously prayed was securely attached, and fell forward onto the roof. Her hands hit the slick surface and she began to slide, but she didn't fall.

*Alex is in so much trouble.* It was that single crisp thought that gave her enough fuel to grab hold of the gable window's eaves and inch forward. The shingles felt as though they'd been coated in vegetable oil, and she slipped her way to the top of the first peak of the gable, where Alex had apparently already spotted her.

She sank to the small crest, sitting on the frigid wetness, and tried to forget she was terrified of heights. "Get over here, young man."

He might not be able to hear her, but he knew good and well what she was saying. He gaped at her from beneath the hood of his coat; he looked wet to the skin. He held up the hammer as if explaining what he was doing on the roof.

The boy meant well. He had a good heart. But this

was dangerous! She crooked her finger, giving him her best imperial look. "Now."

"I'm almost done." She couldn't hear his words, but she could read his lips.

"Move." She gave him her most severe look, the one that meant business.

He tried to charm her with "The Eye," thinking himself so grown up and manly, she reasoned, for being the one to fix the leaking roof. But that was what roofers were for. They were paid to fix roofs. She didn't relent, and finally he gave in and crawled nimbly along the dangerous roof, seemingly without a care in the world. That boy! She grabbed him the second he was in range. "Down. Now."

"Yeah, Mom, that's what I'm doing." He looked amused more than anything as he swung down, using the supports of the covered staircase roof, and landed on the top step.

If only she were that agile! Paige went to follow suit, but she couldn't get any traction as she eased down the protection of the gable window. Just at the time her boots threatened to follow the water and slide right over the full gutters to the ground below, a big male hand shot out from the gray curtain of wind-driven rain.

But it wasn't Alex's hand. It was Evan Thornton in his Sunday best, soaked and looking more handsome than any man had the right to look. Instead of

appearing as a drowned rat, the way she feared *she*
did, the rain slicked his dark hair to his scalp, making him look virile and capable, and when he took
her hand, his touch felt as invincible as steel.

I don't want to like this man, she reminded herself firmly, surprised that she was so glad to see him.
Not that she needed help, no, but his just being near
seemed to take the sting out of the icy rain and the
damp out of the air. She didn't like that, either! She
did not want Evan to affect her in the slightest. But
he did. She could no longer deny it as his hands
gripped hers and held her steady as she crossed from
the roof to the rail and down.

"You didn't need to come rescue me." She didn't
mean to sound harsh.

"I didn't come to rescue you. I saw Alex up there,
as I drove by on my way to church, and I thought he
didn't belong up there. At least, not without someone who knows what they're doing on a roof."

"And that would be you?"

"Sure. I put myself through college working car-
pentry in the summers. Want me to take a look?"

"I want you safe on the ground. That roof is
slick."

"It's a piece of cake." Only then did she realize he'd
grabbed Alex's hammer, which he must have taken
from him on the stairs. "Go inside before you freeze.
Have a hot cup of coffee waiting for me, would you?"

And as if he had the perfect right, he climbed onto the roof and disappeared, as agile as a gorilla. A great big, pushy *male* gorilla. Why she was furious, she couldn't explain it to herself, but she wasn't about to let some man, some arrogant, know-it-all man, think he could rescue her. She didn't need help. She might have appreciated the referral to a good plumber, and though she likely could have gotten herself out of the snowdrift, she appreciated the use of his truck's winch, but *this was way too far.*

This was her roof! She didn't seem to have any trouble, other than a single slip as she cleared the gable, angrily climbing low along the slope of the roof. Rain lashed her. A cruel wind battered her as she knelt beside Evan.

He didn't seem surprised to see her. "I thought you were headed inside."

"You thought wrong. This is my roof. My problem."

"Fine. You want to hold this flush so I can hammer this flashing back down?"

There was a flicker of amusement in his dark eyes, eyes that had flecks of gold and bronze in those brown irises. Expressive eyes that seemed so…caring. Caring. She had to be wrong. Evan Thornton didn't really care about her. She didn't know why he was on her roof, but there was no way he was doing this out of some sense of fairness. Or, maybe he was just after a few free meals. That was easier to believe than the fact that a man could care about her.

She knew for a fact that a man couldn't. Men were undependable. Unreliable. And when Jimmy had left her, the pain had brought her to her knees. She'd loved him. She'd truly loved him. No, she'd been foolish ever to care, even a little, for a man.

That's when a familiar minivan caught her attention as it pulled in at an angle, taking two spots, in front of the diner. Heath emerged from the driver's door, leaving the vehicle running, and bolted onto the sidewalk. With another slam, her eight-year-old nephew followed his new dad into the diner and out of her sight. Heath had come to fetch Amy. The realization was like a terrible twisting sensation in her chest, a twisting that tightened until it felt as if her lungs were being ripped into shreds. *Some* men, she amended, were constant and committed.

"Like this?" She held the edge of the tin flashing firmly, the way he'd been doing it.

He nodded, not even bothering to look at what she was doing. His gaze latched on hers and like a brush to her heart, she felt touched in places she'd never even known were inside her. As if there was an undiscovered room in her heart— There she went, believing in things that weren't real. Things that had no substance or merit. Wishful thinking was a flaw she couldn't afford.

If it was possible, the rain came down in an even fiercer wave, the crashing downpour turning to pebble-sized hail.

"This just isn't getting any easier," Evan chuckled, as if he didn't mind at all. He slid a nail near to her fingertips and gave a competent tap.

Most men grumbled when they were uncomfortable, and squatting on top of a diner's roof in the middle of a hailstorm wasn't anything close to being comfortable. And many men thought they were pretty handy, but they weren't. Evan, true to his word, tacked down the flashing and tugged the shingles back into place competently.

"That ought to hold until the storm's over. Well, unless it gets any worse." He grinned at her through the downpour, and the cold seemed almost bearable.

The thundering storm, the skin-chilling winds, even the cramp developing in her left calf faded until there was only Evan's steady gaze and his sincere grin and his presence brimming through her like the richest honey. It was a sweetness she'd never known and could not explain.

And certainly had the good sense not to believe in.

She felt her chin rise up, and something that felt like an impenetrable titanium shield close around her heart. "I could have hammered that down myself, you know."

"I know. I have complete confidence in you. But seeing as you're going to have dinner with me to-night—"

*"What?"* She couldn't have heard him right. The hail pounded around them, crescendoing, until the only thing louder was the wild jackhammering of her heartbeat. "We're not having dinner tonight."

"You owe me for this, right?"

"Y-yes." She stopped.

Evan watched her pretty rosebud pink lips shaped with whatever she was about to say next, and realized he was right.

Did she also figure out that he intended to make her keep her word? Evan sure hoped so. "I want dinner with you."

She looked shocked. "You do?"

Why on earth would she look so surprised? Even with the residual rainwater streaking down her face and her hair plastered down, she looked amazing. Her features were delicate, and for all the strength she exuded, there wasn't much to her, but she was no frail beauty. She was feminine and soft and caring and it was not diminished by her capable get-things-done approach to life.

Didn't she know how attractive that was to a man like him? Didn't she know that she fascinated him? He resisted the urge to smooth a stray lock of chestnut hair that had tumbled across her cheek, and he realized with a breath-stealing punch to his chest that he wanted to get to know her better.

So he risked his pride and asked her. "Why not? You're single. I'm single. You practically have dinner with me anyway as it is. You're in the general proximity, right?"

"Well, yeah, I guess, but—" No longer so in charge and self-assured, she bit her bottom lip, as if unsure, showing her rare, vulnerable side. "With Amy ill, I can't—"

"Amy doesn't work Sunday evenings." He hoped that was true; he thought it might be. "And you take one night off a week, don't you?"

"Uh, I always take Sunday evenings off, but I work at home. It's when I do the week's books."

As if an excuse was going to work with him. He'd climbed up on this roof in the middle of a Montana spring storm, and it wasn't out of the kindness of his heart or because he had nothing better to do. "You stop to eat supper, right?"

"Well, usually I bring the plate into my office—"

He laid his hand on hers to stop her, and the instant his fingers met hers, a spark snapped like static electricity. Maybe it was something in the air from the storm, or maybe it was something more, like a sign from above. But either way he could not deny the shock of tenderness that rushed into the empty places of his heart. "You can stop for an hour or two and have dinner with me. Or I'm going to tell your sister and your son and everyone you work with that you promised to go out to dinner with me and then broke your promise."

"You wouldn't!"

He wouldn't, but he liked the way she didn't quite believe him. Good, because he would never do anything to hurt her. But when a man was standing on the peak of a roof with hail getting bigger by the minute and what looked like a thunderstorm on the way, he used what leverage he could. "So, how about I pick you up at your place around six?"

"I—" She intended to argue, to turn him down flat, he could see it. But then something on the sidewalk below stopped her.

He saw her sister Amy walking arm in arm with her new husband, her head leaning on his shoulder. Her little boy hurried ahead to open the passenger door, and there was no mistaking the protective concern on Heath Murdock's granite face as he settled his wife onto the front seat.

Paige shook her head, as if changing her mind on what she'd been about to say, and a lovely brightness swept across her face, turning her cheeks pink and her eyes full of what looked like hope. "If you're so determined to come by and take me to dinner, is there any way I can stop you?"

"Absolutely not." He saw clearly what she couldn't say. Well, there was a lot he couldn't say to her right now either.

He cared about her, and he leaned in close to gather her free hand with his. "Let's get off this roof before lightning decides to barbecue us."

"You know what they say about lightning striking twice?"

He remembered that night's storm. The sparkle of humor in her beautiful blue eyes made him grin, and he felt happy inside, not superficially, but really happy in a way he hadn't felt in so long…he couldn't remember when.

While he'd promised himself he'd never do this again, never open his heart up to the kind of devastation Liz had brought him, he *had* to know if Paige was true all the way down deep.

He led the way down the roof and onto the outside stairwell, never once letting go of her.

# Chapter Ten

"**M**om, where's Mr. Thornton?" Alex popped his head out of the diner's back door, ignoring the golf-ball-sized hail that was driving into them both.

"He went back to his car, I imagine, on his way to church." Bruised and battered and wet clear through from the weather, she tried to ignore the fact that her son might have very easily spotted Evan Thornton helping her off the roof. And holding her hand longer than necessary. Like all the way down the stairs.

She told herself Evan had been worried about her safety, after all, the steps were slick and coated with hail. But secretly it had been *nice*, something unexpected.

"What about you? You've got—" she glanced at the wall clock, "five minutes to make it to the ten o'clock service."

"But the roof—"

"Is no place for you to be in a storm, young man, but church is. So go, but you drive carefully."

"I know." He rolled his eyes, giving her a grin and "The Eye," thinking himself so charming.

Okay, he was. She was biased and, as she'd been since she'd first feasted her eyes on him, totally in love with him. She couldn't help smoothing his wet bangs out of his eyes. "Think you can come back and bus tables for me?"

"Sure. But you know what?" He grabbed his sodden jacket from the hook. Uncaring of the dampness, he thrust his arms into the garment. "You could hire someone else. You know, 'cause you're short-staffed."

"When I find someone reliable, I will." Reliable was a problem when the wage for starting help was the state's minimum, and mostly kids wanted the job. "You're reliable and even cheaper."

His charming grin widened. "You know who's even more reliable than me?"

"I hate to ask."

"Beth. She works over at the drive-in, but she doesn't get enough hours there. And plus, she'd make more here because of tips, right?"

Boy, he sure could pick a sensitive subject, couldn't he? "I don't think it's a good idea to have your girlfriend work here. What if you two break up?

You'd still have to bus when we're short-handed, and you'd have to see her—"

"It's not like that, Mom." He shocked her by smacking a kiss on her cheek. "Beth has to take care of her mom and sister. Her mom's drinking is bad again."

Paige felt a punch of sympathy hit her hard in the chest. She, too, knew what it was like for a teenager to have to carry adult responsibilities. "I don't know. Let me think about it."

"Think all you want. Then hire her." Alex jingled his keys as he grabbed the doorknob. "Hire her, and I won't say one word about you and Mr. Thornton."

With a suggestive waggle of his eyebrows, he was gone, racing into the storm before she could haul him back and set him straight.

You and Mr. Thornton. Alex had said it as if she and Evan were a pair, a couple, who were *dating*. Oh, that boy so had it wrong.

Isn't that what dinner with a man was, a date? a little voice inside her head asked. And didn't that mean she was technically dating Evan Thornton?

It was one date. Just one.

She grabbed the cordless phone and dialed Amy's number. While she waited for the call to connect, she grabbed a dishtowel and dried the rain from her face.

"Hello, Paige." Amy sounded weak and shaky. "I suppose you know what I'm about to say."

"You took a pregnancy test and it's positive?"

"Yep. Since Heath is a doctor, I suppose the result is about as accurate as we're going to get today." She gave a watery sigh. "I've wanted this so badly, but I wasn't like this with Weston."

"Remember how sick I was with Alex?" Paige understood morning sickness all too well. But she'd always wanted another little baby. Even now, the pangs of it tugged at her, but that time in her life had gone the moment her husband had called it quits. "I know Heath is already taking excellent care of you. Congratulations, sweetie."

"Th-thank you." Amy sobbed, a result of happy tears.

It was a happiness Amy deserved. Paige had done her best to make sure her brother and younger sisters had a good life. It hadn't been easy for a teenager to raise kids only slightly younger than she was, but everything she'd done, how hard she'd worked, how hard she'd championed them, was for this, a good and happy life for them.

"I'm taking you off the schedule," Paige decided. "You stay home this week and take good care of yourself and my little niece or nephew."

"Paige, that's great of you, but we can't afford it. Heath is still working that intern position and—"

"I wasn't planning on taking you off the payroll. I just want you to take it easy. We'll square up later, okay? First things first."

"Oh." More tears had her sniffing. "You are a great big sister. I don't think there's a better one on this planet."

"Yeah, yeah. I'm sure you could find about a billion. I'll send one of the twins over with meals for the rest of the day. That way no one needs to worry about cooking, okay? Take it easy. Oh, that's call-waiting. I have to go."

After Amy's grateful goodbye, Paige answered the other call. Probably a business call. It was. A reservation coming in for the brunch. She scribbled the Corey family's name into the book, giving them the last available table.

At least business was picking up, she thought, as she went to look in on the twins. Brandilyn looked busy refilling coffee and passing out copies of the Sunday paper.

See? At least something was normal. It was going to be like any other Sunday. She'd concentrate on the cooking, hand over the dining room to Jodi when she arrived, and refuse to give a single thought to Evan Thornton…and their impending date.

Because it wasn't a real date. Not really.

The congregation was standing for the last chorus of the opening hymn as Evan slipped into the back row. He looked like he'd been drowned and beaten, and he was thankful for an inconspicuous spot. The weather must have discouraged a lot of people from coming, so that meant he had plenty of room and he didn't have to worry about dripping all over perfectly dry worshipers.

Just as the pastor was warming up to his sermon, the back door whispered open and Paige's son sauntered down the aisle, dripping wet, and slipped into a pew next to several kids from the youth group.

That made him think of Cal. While the emptiness from missing his boys was still as sharp as ever, he didn't feel quite so alone. And, remembering the way Paige's hand had felt so right in his, he felt…hopeful for the future.

Someone slunk behind the last row and stopped behind him. "Dad, what happened to you?" whispered a familiar voice.

Cal! There the boy was, looking mighty proud of himself, and taller, wider through the shoulder. He'd grown over the last few months, a man and no longer the little boy Evan was so used to protecting. "Just a little rain," he whispered back. "You didn't tell me you were coming home."

"I thought I'd surprise you, and then I couldn't find you here. I was just about to come looking for you."

"Sit and listen to the minister." He was still the dad; he couldn't help himself.

Cal gave him a sheepish grin, as if he were indulging his old man, slid over the arm of the pew and dropped onto the seat.

It wasn't until the closing hymn that they could manage to talk again.

"Are you staying for brunch?" Evan whispered as the first verse rang around them.

"I'm starvin'. Thought I'd come home with you, well, after we eat, and use the washer and dryer. It's a bummer to use the dorm machines. I never have enough quarters."

"Sure you can use my machines, but it'll cost you two bucks a load. That's a bargain."

"Ha ha. You're hysterical, Dad. You know I came home to bum more money, right?"

"Right. I was a college kid once too, long ago." He resisted the urge to grab his boy in a wrestling hold, mainly because they were in church and because Cal was no longer his boy.

No, he was nineteen years old. He was a man. But, Evan thought as he followed his son down the aisle and out of the church, he will always be my son. He was glad of that fact. Like his older brother, Cal was getting top grades, he made good decisions, was active in church and in sports and behaved well. Evan was proud of his sons, and glad he was in a position to help them get a better start in life than he'd had.

"I'll meet you at the diner." He left Cal next to his

bright red Mustang, a present for graduating with a perfect G.P.A. The vehicle was polished and spotless beneath the layer of sloppy ice that had been obviously falling for a while.

Evan scraped his truck windshield and huddled shivering in the cab while the traffic jammed as it always did on the trek from the church parking lot to the main street. Through the dissipating fog on his windows as his defroster blew hot air, he could see across the town park to Paige's diner.

How was he going to tell Cal about Paige? It was a date, just a date, but there was no way to minimize the significance of it. Evan had never dated while he'd been responsible for the boys; even if he'd had the inclination, he never would have had the time. More than that, though, the boys were not only hurt by the divorce, but they saw up close what their mother had done. The financial disaster was only part of it. Evan knew it was years before he managed to smile again. Longer still until he could laugh, but never had he been the same man.

How was he going to explain he wanted to take a chance again? He couldn't even rationalize it to himself. Then again, it was only a first date. The first step toward a relationship, and it was too soon to tell how things would work out.

Maybe he would wait to tell his boys; after all, he thought as he found a parking spot along the curb, he didn't expect them to tell him every time they went on a date.

The second he pushed through the diner's front door and spotted Cal talking with Paige's son, he knew the decision was out of his hands. The boys had known each other through sports, church and school, of course, and Evan tried to hold hope that the kids were talking about one of those subjects.

But as he approached, he noticed Alex's gaze widen with an uh-oh! expression and water sloshed out of the pitcher he was carrying around.

"Hi there, Mr. Thornton," Alex cleared his throat. "You, uh, want some coffee?"

"I do." And those two words sent the boy hurrying off as if Evan had barked an order. He tried to ignore his son's smirk. "After you surrender possession of my washer and dryer, are you gonna hang around for a while? Or are you heading back to the dorm?"

"I was gonna head straight back. I've got this killer chem test tomorrow, but—" That smirk turned troublesome. "I've decided to stay and help my dad get ready for his date."

*I should have known this would happen.*

Evan was desperately grateful that Alex showed up with a pot of coffee. He was in such a hurry to figure out what to say to his son—and now to Paige's—that he pushed the cup and saucer closer to Alex with a little too much power and the cup rocked toward the edge of the table.

Alex caught it. "Whoa, there. Don't go breaking the dishes, Mr. Thornton, or my mom'll call off the date."

The boys thought that was hilarious by the looks they were exchanging.

"Just pour the coffee." He tried to sound unaffected. They were teenaged boys. They could laugh. What did they know? He was a man; he could sit here and pretend nothing bothered him. At least Cal was taking the news well.

"Your mom won't call off the date. I caught her looking at my dad through the window. She was smiling. Dad is a good catch. I've been worrying about him now that I'm out of the house. He needs someone to keep an eye on him."

"Funny." Evan was glad that Alex had the manners to stay quiet as he filled Cal's cup and then backed away. "A chem test, you said?"

"That's old news. This thing with Paige. How long have you been dating her? She's old, but she's pretty. Hey, she's, like, as old as you!" As if proud of his brilliant deduction, Cal upended the sugar canister over his steaming cup of coffee and stirred.

"I feel so much better now." Evan stood, taking his plate with him. "I'm not that old."

"Of course not," Cal concurred diplomatically.

"But you're, like, forty, Dad. Just roll with it. You don't look all that bad."

"I'm relieved to know that." That was perspective, he thought remembering that when he'd been Cal's age, how anyone older than thirty had seemed ancient. "I figure I'll try to enjoy what life is left me before the rest of my looks go."

"Ha ha, Dad." Cal stepped into the buffet line behind him. "I'm just sayin' you don't need to feel like Mrs. McKaslin won't think you're, you know—"

"Old?" Evan asked wryly as he grabbed a pair of tongs and loaded up on link sausages. "That's the last time I want to hear that word, boy."

"Okay, I wasn't gonna say it, though. I was gonna say ugly."

"Thanks for the words of encouragement. I'm glad I can count on my son at a time like this."

"You can count on me, Dad," Cal shoved his plate at him. "And can I have lots of sausages?" He was already using his free hand to pilfer the piles of crispy bacon. "So, you got reservations for tonight?"

"I don't need my son to help me plan my date." Evan finished doling out sausages and moved onto the choices of hashed or butter-fried potatoes. He took some of both. "I know how to take a woman to dinner."

"Dad, the last lady you dated was Mom. You're out of practice. Times have changed."

"What's changed? You go to dinner, be polite, have conversation and take her home."

"Not so much, Dad." Apparently a dating expert, Cal took over the spoon and loaded diced potatoes next to his mountain of breakfast meat. "You've got to have this all figured out. You don't want her to think this is no big deal."

"Well, it's a first date." And a really big deal, Evan was beginning to realize and didn't want to admit, even to himself. So he chose eggs Benedict over the Belgian waffles and tried not to think about it.

He waited while Cal took both choices, his plate nearly ready to collapse under the weight of all that food, and they headed back to their table together. "I was going to take her to that steak place in Bozeman that we like."

"That's a good place." Cal dropped onto his chair and bowed his head for a quick prayer. As soon as "Amen" was muttered, he grabbed his fork and dug in. "If I were you, I'd pick an even better place. Classier. Mrs. McKaslin's pretty swift. She'll like something real nice."

"That place is nice."

"Yeah, but you're serious, so you have to let her know right up front."

"I never said I was serious."

"Dad, look at her." Cal gestured to the cash register where Paige greeted the newly arrived Corey family. Three generations of them crowded around the counter, as Paige chatted amicably with Mrs. Corey.

Paige. Her loveliness stunned him. Evan couldn't explain what happened in his heart as he looked at her. Yes, she was sure something. It had taken him a decade to notice, but he was finally ready, and he *was* noticing.

She'd changed into dry clothes, something she might have had on hand, he suspected, for the jeans peering out from beneath her crisp ruffled green apron were wash-worn, and it was a high-school sweatshirt she wore. Her hair was curlier than usual, probably from the rain and wind, and every time he looked at her she became more beautiful. Not in a cool, distant kind of way, but he noticed warmth and heart in her that he'd never taken the time to notice before.

His son's words haunted him. Serious. Am I serious about her?

How could he not be?

"Look, Dad, a friend of mine works at this great restaurant in Bozeman. I'll give her a call, get you a cool table, and on the way home we'll stop by and get some flowers."

"Flowers?" He had a hard time focusing on anything because Paige was coming his way, leading the

Corey family down the aisle, chatting with Mrs. Corey over her shoulder as she went. Paige was elegance and she fascinated him.

On the way past his table, she surprised him by flashing him a warm knowing smile. One that made his soul lurch. One that made him feel alive all over again.

"Dad? You are one sorry dude. But it's gonna be okay. I'm gonna take care of you. Help you out with this."

Evan tried to focus on his son and had a hard time doing it. "Help? Nah, I got this all wrapped up. You need to study for your chem test."

"Dad." Cal shook his head like a parent who knows best when confronting a clueless teenager. "You have *so* much to learn. It's a good thing you have me. Who knew all my dating expertise was going to pay off? Now, what is it you're always telling me? Respect the girl. Mind your manners. Be a gentleman. I don't have to tell you what that means, do I?"

Evan felt his face burn. "No, I think we can safely say that I'll be a perfect gentleman. Let me think. I'm trying to remember why I was glad you came home? All that quiet I've been enjoying sounds good about now."

"Yeah, yeah. Face it, Dad. You need me." Cal stuffed a forkful of waffle into his mouth, enjoying this way too much.

Evan's gaze roamed across the dining room to where Paige was helping elderly Mrs. Corey into a chair and when Mr. Corey insisted that was his job, Paige simply melted.

In that brief moment he saw something new about her. Paige McKaslin was an old-fashioned girl.

Well, she was in luck, because he was a hold-the-door, treat-a-woman-right, old-fashioned kind of guy.

# *Chapter Eleven*

"Mom, you're gonna be late for your date!" Alex's voice echoed down the long hallway. "Mom!"

"I'm in here." She checked her reflection in the big beveled mirror over her dresser.

The woman who gazed back at her looked ready for a meal at a fine restaurant. Her hair was tidy, her jewelry sedate—except for her earrings, maybe those were too much. And maybe the black rayon jacket and pants set made her look too severe. She had time. She should pick something else. There was that pretty pink dress she'd worn at Easter, and it had been a flattering color on her.

No, I'm not going to be one of those women who dress to suit some man, she told herself firmly. This is just dinner. Just a thank-you for all he's done. He's a customer. He's a man. He's not really interested in me.

But am I interested in him? She couldn't quite answer that question truthfully, and she was glad for the interruption of her son bounding through her open bedroom door, looking windswept and bright-eyed. "What have you been up to?"

"No good." With a wide grin, he dropped into the overstuffed chair by the picture window. "You know me. Robbing banks. Holding up old ladies."

"Sure. Did you play basketball at the church?"

"When it finally stopped raining. I told Beth to stop by the diner tomorrow on her way to school. She has work release so she doesn't have to be there until noon."

"I never said I'd hire her." Paige decided black was the perfect color for a woman with a teenage son who had a girlfriend. The perfect color for a woman who was not going to believe in love again. The perfect color to remind her that this dinner wasn't a genuine date. "And before you say anything, I am short-handed, but I can't hire her just because you like her."

"There's a reason I like her, Mom. She's a good person." Her teenaged boy flashed her a telling look. "Isn't that what you always say is important?"

Paige rolled her eyes. "Aren't you supposed to be doing something? Your homework, maybe?"

"Yeah, yeah, I'll get to it. What I need to do—" he rose up to his full six-foot height, "is help my mommy get ready to go out with her new boyfriend."

That he seemed pleased with the idea only made her laugh. Laughing covered up her embarrassment. She snapped the back off her left earring. "If I ever hear you say *boyfriend* again, you'll be grounded so fast, it'll make your head spin."

"Ooh, I'm afraid." With a wink he caught her hand. "Leave the earrings. They're pretty. Just like you."

Her heart melted. "You stop trying to charm me."

"It's just the truth, Mom." Sincerity shone in his eyes, as blue as hers, when their gazes met in the mirror. "Cal told me his dad's like *waaay* serious about you. And I figure, this'll be good for ya. Get out. Be with a nice guy your own age. I raised ya right. I trust ya."

Before she could begin to figure out what on earth she should say to that, the doorbell chimed. Nerves skidded through her like cold ice. Her fingertips felt frozen as if she'd been hours out in the cold and she had a tough time getting the earring back on.

"That'll be him." With a delighted grin, Alex dashed from the room.

Paige gripped the edge of the dresser, holding on for dear life as her son's words replayed in her head. *Cal told me his dad's like* waaay *serious about you.*

That can't be right, can it? Paige clicked on the earring back. *And if it is, oh, Lord, what am I going to do?* Because she had mentally prepared herself to have a friendly conversation over a meal with Evan. To keep her shields up and her hopes, as tiny as they were, securely in place. What she wasn't ready for was a big first step on a path that was uncertain and risky.

No, she told herself firmly, Alex's words were nothing more than the result of two boys speculating on their parents' relationship. It was nothing to worry about. She took a steadying breath, heard the front door close and the rumble of male voices in conversation. It looked like Evan was waiting for her, so she grabbed her evening bag and headed down the hall. She was ready for a casual, friendly dinner. She wouldn't think about the rest.

"Evan." His name spilled from her lips at the sight of the fit and handsome man standing in her foyer, wearing a striking black suit and coordinating black tie, and holding a vase of long-stemmed red roses. There were so many perfect buds, she could smell the beautiful old-fashioned aroma as she stumbled the last few yards down the hallway. "Oh, you brought flowers."

"You like 'em?"

"Y-yes. Thank you." The flowers were exquisite, but it was the man who captivated her. The man whose dark eyes widened with visible appreciation as she stepped into the fall of the overhead light. His was no casual look, but one that frightened her for all its sincerity and warmth. She saw the man's steady heart and kind nature in the slow sweep of his smile.

"Paige. You look beautiful."

The way he said it, made her think that he believed it. She couldn't remember any man who'd ever said that to her. It wasn't true, and she couldn't let herself read anything into his misguided belief, but deep down, it mattered. She knew she was beaming as she smiled at him. "You brought me flowers?"

"I was told by my son it is important to make the right impression. How am I doing?"

Wonderful. "Passable."

Alex stepped in to take the flowers. "That means she's pleased. You two have a nice time. Drive safe. Oh, and Mom, don't forget you have a curfew."

"You are enjoying this way too much, young man." Her hand shook as she reached into the hall closet for her Sunday-best coat. "I want all your homework done before you turn on the TV."

"Roger, captain." He disappeared into the kitchen. "Call if you're gonna be late. You know the rules."

Thank heavens for her son. She was chuckling instead of trembling as she slipped her arm into her coat sleeve and missed. She was rattled, that was all. More nervous than she expected to be. The evening had turned more serious than she had imagined.

"Let me." Evan was there, a big powerful presence behind her, holding her coat so she could try again. He was so close she could smell the pleasant spice of his aftershave. She felt small next to him, feminine and womanly, something she hadn't felt in so long. It was as if a part of her was awakening, and there was more light for her eyes to see by and more heart for her to feel alive.

Evan settled the coat around her shoulders with care. "Since you have a curfew, we'd best get going."

The low rumble of humor in his voice seemed to draw her closer. "I noticed Cal was with you at the diner. What does he think of this?"

Evan held the door for her. "I didn't get a curfew, but I have to call him with a report as soon as I get home. He tried to give me advice. He thought I needed it."

"Do you?"

"Considering I haven't dated for two whole decades, I think that's a yes." Evan shut the door and followed her down the steps. "Cal gave me advice all day long. When he stopped, Phil called in with even more advice."

"So, how does everyone know about this?"

Evan opened the passenger door for her. "I'm sure my son is to blame. I'll beat him thoroughly the next time I see him."

"Yeah, I'm sure you will." Paige didn't look as if she believed it for a second.

And she would be right. He took her elbow as she climbed up into the cab, and he could feel her muscles tense beneath the layers of clothes. She was small-boned, hardly anything at all to her, he realized, and a hard surge swelled through him, bringing with it the need to protect her. To take care of her.

Strong needs for so early in the game. He didn't trust feelings, and so he did his best to hold them back as he closed her door and circled around to the driver's side.

He had to be careful. This was how it had all gone wrong with Liz, or at least that was his theory. He'd been overwhelmed with those strong male traits to love and protect. Liz wanted to be taken care of and he wanted to love and protect her.

He'd fallen too hard too fast, and he hadn't noticed the small signs and clues along the way until she had his ring on her finger and it was way too late to step back.

He had to tread carefully. He would not make that mistake again.

Had she ever been so nervous in her entire life? If she had, Paige couldn't remember when. It wasn't like her at all. She was never rattled. She was a single parent, a business owner and responsible for her employee's salaries every month. She couldn't afford to be anything but rock-solid.

It was Evan. He was putting her right out of her comfort zone.

And to make matters worse, he kept getting the doors for her. Didn't he know she was perfectly capable of getting them for herself?

She walked through the heavy wood-and-glass doors to one of the nicest restaurants in the area. Evan's hand settled on her shoulder as he followed her into the lobby. The lights were low, and restful piano music added a tasteful background. The décor was Western and expensive.

Nice place. A fire crackled in the central stone fireplace in the dining area of high-backed booths and the firelight reflected in the long row of windows that overlooked the spectacular mountains.

A hostess tended to them immediately and Paige managed what she hoped was a composed appearance as she followed the college-age girl past the fireplace to a window table. Tucked in the corner, it was cozy and private and offered a stunning view of the up close Bridger Peaks and the rugged Rocky Mountains. The pewter sky was swept with broad strokes of magenta and gold from the setting sun.

Evan had pulled out all the stops. There was no possible way she could call this a casual friendly meal, not considering this elegant restaurant. He held out a chair for her, indicating she should take the better view. Wordless, she slipped into the chair and the solid warmth of his presence so undeniably close had her trembling all over again.

She wasn't prepared for this. Not at all. But she didn't want to stop it from happening, either.

Evan seated himself across the table, and while she accepted the menu from the hostess and tried to concentrate on the specials, she felt as if the room were spinning. Alex's words kept replaying in her head. *Cal told me his dad's like* waaay *serious about you.* Why had the boy told her that? She didn't want to hear things like that! She felt as if she were standing on the edge of a tall cliff with the earth crumbling away around her feet.

As soon as the hostess stepped away from their table, Evan leaned closer. "Did you happen to catch what she was saying?"

"No," she confessed. "I was too blown away by the view to listen very well."

Not exactly the truth, but she didn't feel comfortable confessing just how anxious she was. Would he understand? He looked sure and confident, as always. The menu he held open in his wide, capable hands was steady, unlike hers. This dating thing is for the birds, she decided. Why on earth would anybody do this to themselves?

Evan studied her with a small smile, as if he had a secret. "The view? I didn't notice. All I can see is you."

The air evaporated from her lungs. Her heart forgot to beat. Thought fled from her poor befuddled brain. This was not friendship; this was not safe ground. The earth was crumbling faster around her metaphorical feet, and she didn't like knowing she was about to fall.

"Cal said the steaks here are great." Evan kept talking, his tone calm and steady and everything a dream man should be. "That's not the exact words. I think he said they were awesome."

Their boys. This was safe ground; safe conversation. She groped for what normalcy she could. "How is your son liking MSU?"

"Cal's thriving. Busy. Wasn't homesick for a minute. He got a good roommate in the dorms, and he's made friends. I think he manages to study in there some time. Actually, he's doing well. Growing up and away."

"Kids tend to do that. Alex is going to be spending the summer working as a camp counselor up near Glacier National Park. And so after this graduation, I'll be sending him off into the world. Now that it's getting closer, I don't think I'm going to like that as much as I always thought."

"I know what you mean. I raised my boys to be good men. They are. I'm proud of them. But they were my life."

"As they should be." They had this in common.

Not only were they the ones in their marriages who had stayed the course, they were also the ones who had had the reward of spending their lives day by day with their children.

That's what real love was, the holding on when it was hard to do so. Evan had a steadfast heart. And, after feeling the sting of a husband who'd bailed, there was nothing more important to her in a man.

A perky waitress arrived, obviously a college girl from the nearby campus, who introduced herself as Caitlin. Fortunately, she repeated the specials for Evan, who considered the choices and indicated that Paige should order first.

She chose the smallest steak, thinking the less food, the quicker the meal would be finished and the sooner she could get this over with. A suffocating ache had dug in deep in the center of her chest. An ache that was pure emotion, a little of the past hurting, and mostly fears she could not put into words. They were fears she didn't want to acknowledge.

While Evan ordered one of the evening's special Angus steaks, Paige watched the sunset. The pewter clouds turned nearly purple as the last of the light burned into the glacial peaks of the Rockies. It was stunningly beautiful, but she felt a little like that sun slipping into the unseen beyond and treading in unfamiliar country.

Relationships—even a first date—required vulnerability. Exposing an honest piece of who you really are to another person. She'd done that once, and gotten burned where she was most fragile. She'd decided long ago that nothing—*nothing*—could ever be worth the risk of hurting like that.

Except one thing.

As Paige reached for her water, her attention caught and held on the couple one table over, just visible some distance behind Evan. They were in their retirement years, seated together on the same side of the table, leaning toward one another instead of away.

How sweet. The wife gazed up at her husband with honest adoration, and her husband took her delicate hand and kissed her knuckles tenderly, the sconce light reflecting on the slim gold wedding ring she wore.

A great love. Wasn't that what every girl dreamed of finding one day? It hadn't happened to her; she believed that it could not. But she'd seen plenty of people who seemed to have marriages that worked. And some couples had something more, something special. That true love was so special and rare, it had to be like holding on to a little piece of heaven.

"That's really something, isn't it?" She hadn't realized Evan had finished speaking with the waitress, who had turned out, apparently, to be a friend of his son's. Embarrassed to be caught watching something that was so private, she reached for her water goblet. "It's heartening to see that some marriages really last," he continued.

She nodded, for that was just what she had meant to say. "It's so easy to see the bad divorces and the painful marriages and love that has broken apart."

"Especially when that's what happened to you." Evan's deep baritone resonated with understanding. "What happened to Alex's father?"

"He decided he'd had enough of responsibility and left in the middle of the breakfast rush." Her hand was trembling again and she tried to still it as she lifted the water glass. Somehow she managed to get a sip of water down without choking.

"No," Evan said gently. "What really happened?"

*I don't want to tell you what really happened.* Her hand wobbled. She set down the goblet before she dropped it. "No one knows that story. It's not very interesting."

"I'm interested."

Her heart gave a lurch. She'd never been so glad to see a waitress. Caitlin arrived with their house salads, with ranch dressing for her and Italian for Evan and ground fresh pepper, giving Paige enough time to prepare herself. While time had dulled the pain, the scars had gone deep. All the way down to her soul.

She'd never told anyone the truth. She didn't know if she could open up so much now.

Instead of taking up his salad fork, Evan laid his big, warm hand over hers.

His touch was as unsettling as it was comforting, because she was used to neither. She'd been alone in the most essential way for so long, the connection of his hand on hers felt like everything she could ever want and at the same moment everything she was afraid of. "There's not much to tell. I married Jimmy when I was nineteen and he was twenty. We thought we were in love.

"But in a year's time, I was pregnant, there had been a kitchen fire in the diner and we were in debt up to our ears from the repairs. I was raising Amy and Rachel; Ben was in and out of trouble and acting out. I had more responsibility than I could handle, and Jimmy just had enough one day. He walked out with half our morning regulars listening to us argue. That's it."

Technically, her story was correct. But it left out the real things, the painful arguments and disappointments that she did not want to remember. Because if she did remember what love had brought her, then she would also remember how she'd vowed never to go through that devastation again.

"That's not it. You loved him."

She knew that surprise showed on her face. "I was too young to know what love is. I thought he was something he wasn't. It was my mistake."

"You thought he was the kind of man who stayed, even when the better turned to worse?"

She swallowed hard. *The truth, Paige.* Evan had asked for the truth, and he was waiting patiently, the silent demand of his touch seeped into her like the heat from his skin on hers. She studied his hand, his knuckles were thick but not beefy, his fingers well-proportioned and so capable looking. He knew the unspeakable sadness of a failed marriage. Of a broken love.

She was going to trust that he would understand. "I thought he loved me enough to stay. Until I found out he didn't love me at all. Not really. He just wanted someone to take care of him. You know, do his laundry, put a roof over his head and food on the table. He said that I was good at taking care of other people. It's what I do. And he was right. I think that's what hurt the most."

She tried to tug her hand free.

He held on tight. "I've been there, too. Liz went from her parents' house to her college dorm at her school to marrying me. She'd had a sheltered childhood, and she was looking to be taken care of. It was my mistake, because I was looking for a real helpmate in a wife, in a best friend."

"I thought that's what marriage was."

"Me, too." Evan couldn't explain why, but he could feel her truth like the bright cast of light from the setting sun on his face. In a blinding moment, he understood. She'd been raising her younger brother and sisters, running a business on her own, responsibilities he'd never had at that age, and she'd been looking for a man. Had hoped that's what her husband would be. The same as he'd done with his wife. "Being let down like that, why, it does something to a person."

"Yes." She shook out her napkin, hand trembling, and turned to stare longingly out the window.

Was she dreaming of escaping him, he wondered, or was it escape from remembering the past? She'd said yes to the date; she must want to be here. But that didn't make it any easier to risk trusting him. He knew that. "I want you to know up front, that I've never intentionally let someone down in my life. Just so you know."

He released her hand then. "Do you want to say grace? Or do you want me to do the honor?"

"Y-you." Paige cleared her throat, thankful she was able to get that one word out. Her throat felt as if it had closed shut and she knew she'd never be able to say a blessing. He'd gone and said the one thing that mattered the most. "N-neither have I. Let anyone d-down."

As the last ray of sun slid behind the Rockies, the twilight and shadows lengthened everywhere but in her heart.

## *Chapter Twelve*

Paige felt a mix of relief and regret when Evan turned his truck into her driveway. Clouds blotted out any starlight, and the night stretched black and ominous as the headlights slashed twin paths through the dark woods. A movement blurred just beyond the reach of the light.

"My horse is out."

Evan saw it, too, and braked to a sudden stop just in time. The shadowed movement became an Arabian that bolted across the road, turning golden in the beam of the headlights.

"That mare." Paige rolled her eyes and popped open the door. "You can just leave me here. I've got to get her."

"You've got to be kidding." Evan shifted into Park and set the parking brake. "Didn't I tell you at dinner? I'm not the kind of man who bails."

I've noticed. Paige didn't want to feel the tug of appreciation that made her throat ache and burn. It was easier just to hop out into the gusting wind and night and feel her good shoes squish in the mud on the shoulder of the graveled driveway.

She heard Evan's door close as she wrapped her coat around her and called out to the mare poised in the middle of the road like a deer caught in the headlights. "Annie, baby. Did you get your stall door open again?"

The mare's nostrils flared as she scented Evan.

"Do you want me to herd her toward you?" he called from the other side of the truck.

"No, she's just having some fun. Baby, come with me." Mud sucked at her shoes as she approached, hands out, palms up.

The mare pressed her nose into those hands and her head against Paige's stomach. Spotlighted by the headlights in shades of gold and platinum, woman and horse came together, a revealing moment as she rubbed her mare's long nose. The animal's trust and affection for her mistress was unmistakable. As was the realization that hit him. He was short a horse-riding partner.

Paige rode horses.

"Hey, girl." Her voice was tender and her slender hands gentle as she grasped the nylon halter the mare wore. "Evan, I'm just going to walk her up to the stable. Thank you for an unexpected evening."

"Unexpected, what does that mean?"

"I mean that I'm glad you asked me."

As if shy that she'd said too much, Paige dipped her head, turned her back and hurried down the driveway. The big mare at her side ambled with her, her hooves crunching in the gravel.

*She's glad she went out with me.* Slow joy spread through Evan as he hopped back inside the cab and put the truck in first gear. There was a lot to like about Paige, the private woman who kept her real self well hidden, but he'd seen the part of her she protected so well.

Her confession came back to him, what she'd said when she'd spoken of her husband's betrayal. *He said that I was good at taking care of other people. It's what I do. And he was right. I think that's what hurt the most.* But who had taken care of her through the years? Had anyone?

It was amazing, too, that she was the one woman he just might be able to trust. A woman who'd been through something similar. Who'd been hurt in the same way. A woman with a gentle heart and a kind spirit who made him want to hold her…just to hold her.

The road curved, and Paige and her horse veered off through a path in the trees. He put the truck into

Park and hopped out to help with the gate that gleamed just within the faint reaches of the headlights, but it was already open.

"Did you get that untied all on your own?" Paige didn't even seem annoyed as the mare disappeared into the paddock.

He waited while the first drops of cold rain pelted him on the head. He waited while the drops became steadier and by the time Paige had emerged from the dark shadows, he was wet clean through. But he didn't mind. He opened her door, so she could hop inside.

"Evan, I'm muddy. I don't want to get your interior dirty."

"It's happened before. And this date isn't over until I see you to your door."

"Isn't that an old-fashioned rule?"

"Sometimes old-fashioned is the best." He tucked her hand in his, and the connection that zinged through him hit him right in the soul.

*Please let her be all that I think she is, Lord.*

It had been a long time since he'd wanted anything so much. His spirit ached with the power of it. They'd had a solid conversation over dinner about their kids, their jobs and their church. They'd lived in the same town all their lives; there were plenty of things to discuss, from the yearly Founder's Day celebration to the fundraiser for the county library Paige was catering.

And as Evan cupped her elbow to help her into the truck, he felt something greater than he'd ever felt before: a tender desire to take care of this woman who worked so hard. His feelings were moving way too fast for his brain. He needed to take his time. Neither of them was in a hurry. Love was best, he'd learned, when it was meant to be instead of when it was rushed into being.

He made sure she was in and gave her seatbelt a tug so she wouldn't have to search for it, before shutting the door. He'd never expected the evening to turn out so well. He'd never expected to feel an emotional connection so strong. He didn't know why it was there, but he figured it made sense in a way.

He'd always known Paige, from a distance to be sure, but she was everything he admired in a woman.

Tonight had only shown him she was even more amazing on a deeper level.

They drove the rest of the way in silence. The hum of the heater and the rhythm of the wiper blades were deafening. Evan knew he wanted to ask Paige for another date. The question was, would she say yes? It was tough, but he only had a few more moments with her, so he had to gather up his courage now or it would be too late.

He steeled himself, preparing for her rejection. "I hope I wasn't too boring tonight."

He put the truth of what he was thinking right out there for her to comment on. What would her reaction be? He waited the infinitesimal beats between one second and the next.

"Boring?" She turned to him, highlighted by the dash lights enough that he could see the surprise clearly on her lovely face. "I was worrying you thought the same thing about me. I work, I take care of my family, I work some more. That's hardly exciting."

"It is to me." He pulled into the graveled spot next to the house and shifted into Park. "That's just about all I do."

"Don't men at your age have a mid-life crisis? You know, sports cars, excitement, twenty-year-old wives?"

There was a gentle lilt to her words, as if she were kidding him, but he could feel the dead seriousness beneath. "I'm happy with my life. A sports car wouldn't haul my horse trailer. I think a quiet evening reading at home is exciting. And I would only bore a twenty-year-old, aside from the fact that my youngest son is nineteen. That would be beyond wrong."

Okay, that was a good answer, Paige thought while Evan hopped out and circled around the vehicle. Although Jimmy hadn't left her for a mid-life crisis, he'd been having another sort of crisis, and it had left it hard for her to trust any man.

Evan opened her door. "Do you think I got you home before your curfew?"

"It's only nine o'clock. I think I'm safe from my son's wrath." She liked the way he chuckled easily and the sure way he took her hand. She felt as light as air as he accompanied her up the walkway.

Those pesky nerves returned. Did she invite him in? Did she let him kiss her good night?

"About Wednesday evening." Evan stopped on the top step, clearly meaning to leave her by the door. "I'll pick you up at the diner around seven?"

He wanted to see her again. Why did that make her feel like she'd filled up with helium and was about to float away? She was way too practical for romantic foolishness. "I don't remember saying that I would go with you. But then again, I'd hate to be the reason you decided not to go to Bible study."

"Then it's a date." The way he said it, wasn't a question but a confirmation. As was the deliberate step he took in her direction.

Was he going to kiss her? Something between panic and wonder held her locked in place as his mouth slanted over hers. The first brush of his warm lips to hers was the sweetest she'd ever known.

Tenderness filled her like a slow, sweet waltz, and when he moved away into the shadows off the porch, she swore she could hear music.

"Good night, Paige. I'll see you soon." He left her standing in the glow of the porch light, bathed in raindrops and alight with hope.

Max was breathing on the other side of the door, a happy welcome-home pant that, since he was such a big dog, was louder than the rain tapping all around her. She felt wrapped in a warm pure glow, staring into the direction of the idling truck.

A dark figure cut through the headlights, the dome light appeared and disappeared. She spun and bolted through the door. Max was bounding up and down on all fours, his doggy mouth stretched in a happy grin.

She stroked the top of his wide head with her hand. The puppy Alex had begged her for had grown into a one-hundred-and-twenty-three-pound giant, and he was still growing. The sleek, powerful dog took up most of the available space in the foyer, and she had to reach around him to hang her jacket up on the set of hooks by the door.

Only when she saw the streak of mud across the side of the garment did she remember she'd been out in the muddy field. And her shoes were caked with it. She'd completely lost her mind, apparently, and tracked mud into the house.

Great going, Paige. A single kiss was all it took for her to lose control of her good sense.

Oh, well, it had been a lovely evening. And

Evan—why, she really liked him. Too much for her own good. Too much for the safety of her heart. He was a good man, she knew that. But it was a long rocky road to trusting a man enough for…well, whatever lay ahead. If they made it that far. Her future and what direction it was going to take was a big question mark.

As she kicked off her shoes and set them to dry by the heater vent, she saw Alex's light on downstairs. If he was studying, she didn't want to interrupt him. That was her excuse. She really didn't want to interrupt him, because she didn't want to answer any questions about her date.

Not that she could avoid questions forever, but she needed time to make sense of things. Nothing had been what she'd expected tonight. She couldn't remember a time in her adult life when a man had more than exceeded her expectations in every way.

The phone rang. When Alex didn't pick up, she gave away her presence in the house by snatching up the kitchen extension. "Hello?"

"Paige?" Someone was crying—one of the twins. "Paige? Are you, like, really busy right now?"

"Of course not. Where are you? I'll come over."

"N-no." Brianna sobbed, stuttering. "We're almost to y-your house. Mom and Keith got into this b-bad fight—"

Paige ached for the girls. Their mother had married a man who was better at drinking and gambling than at holding down a job, and Paige constantly worried about the girls' welfare. There was only so much she could do, but she did what she could. "Of course, you come right on over. The porch light is on, and I'll whip up some hot chocolate."

"With sp-sprinkles?" she asked through a sob.

"Absolutely. You girls drive safely. Promise?"

"O-okay. Brandilyn's dr-driving. She's, like, way b-better at it than me."

After saying goodbye, Paige left the cordless receiver on the counter and went in search of the special secret recipe cocoa mix she'd brought home from the diner. There was a jar of it somewhere.

"Hey, Mom." Alex startled her. He was in the entryway next to his dog. "Who's coming over?"

"The twins. How's the homework going?"

"It's going. Why are you all muddy?"

"Annie got out again. She figured out how to open the gates. Could you go figure something out to hold her in until the morning?"

"Sure. Oh, I forgot. I need this form thing signed for school tomorrow." He shoved a piece of paper toward her before he dropped into one of the bar chairs on the other side of the counter. "It's for our field trip to the Museum of the Rockies. So, how went the big date?"

"Fine. We had dinner. We talked. We came

home." Paige opened the drawer next to her, pulled a pen out of the organizer, and signed the form. "Is that field trip this week?"

"Friday. You changed the subject."

"No, I was finished telling you about my date." She pulled a saucepan out of the lower cabinet and plunked it on the stove. "Wait, I can see those wheels turning in your brain, so listen up. No, I'm not in love with him. No, I'm not planning on marrying him—"

"He'd be like my stepdad. Never thought I'd get one at my advanced age."

"You can't look into the future. I can't look into the future, so drop it. Are you worried about that, about me marrying one day?"

"Worried? Nah, I'm not worried. I just don't want to go off to college and leave you alone."

"It's your job to grow up and move away. It's mine to make sure that you do—" She took the milk from the fridge and set it on the counter as the doorbell rang. Max barked joyously. "Could you get that dog?"

"He's so well-trained." Alex rolled his eyes, grinned, and jogged to hold the black-masked rott-weiler back so Paige could muscle open the door.

The girls were rain-soaked and tear-stained and in emotional tatters. Setting her thoughts of Evan aside, she helped them carry their overnight bags down the hall to the guest bedroom next to hers, drew each girl a bath in separate bathrooms and got them to soaking.

Such was her life. She took care of others first and didn't get a moment to herself until it was after midnight.

Evan. Just thinking his name lessened the shadows in her soul.

Paige. Evan had thought of little else in the last twenty-two hours.

It had been a typical Monday with disasters by the truckload, but he'd tackled meeting after meeting and one conference phone call after another with unusual efficiency. Nothing had dimmed his happiness. He was in a good mood because he couldn't get Paige out of his mind. Or their kiss.

Tenderness filled him. He pulled his truck to a parking spot in front of the diner and checked his reflection in the visor mirror. His hair was still a little damp from his shower at the gym, but he'd had a good day, a good workout and he was looking forward to a good evening—because he'd be seeing Paige in about two minutes.

The evening was cool and bright as he stepped onto the curb and spotted her through the rose-hued window. Sunset blazed overhead, painting the street with a soft glow, and the light seemed to find Paige in the dining room, falling across her lovely face like a touch from heaven.

*I'm not ready to care so much so soon.*

This was not the take-it-slow, one-step-at-a-time pace that he'd planned. As he pushed through the door and she turned as if she sensed his presence, he felt a click in his heart, like a key turning in a long-unused lock, like a door opening and sunlight flooding inside for the first time. He felt renewed as their gazes locked.

There was no hiding the gleam of warmth that lit her sapphire eyes or the secret quirk of a smile in the corners of her soft mouth. Remembering their kiss, remembering the connection they'd shared last night, he took one step forward and another to his usual seat at the counter.

"I see you found your way here tonight." Paige brought her smile and a menu. "You know the usual Monday specials, and we also have a grilled salmon special."

"So, that's how you're going to greet me, huh?"

She blushed. "Now you want preferential customer treatment? How about a complimentary soda?"

When she looked down at the counter, as if it held some great interest, he could feel as plainly as if the emotions were his own, her shyness. This was new to them both. "I seem to remember how we said goodbye last night."

Her cheeks blushed harder, but there was a twinkle in her eye as she reached for the soda cups. "Oh, and you thought you might get something similar with a hello?"

"A guy can hope."

"This is a place of business, I'll have you know." She filled the cup with ice and then cola. "If it's not on the menu, then it's not served."

Okay, he had a sense of humor, too. "So, what do I have to do? Ask for a rain check?"

"Maybe." She slipped the beverage on the counter in front of him. "I'll be back. The twins are not having a good day."

"Is there anything I can do to help you?"

His question took Paige by surprise. He wanted to help her? *Evan, I'm going to fall so hard in love with you if you keep saying things like that to me.*

The pathway was so familiar, she could probably do an entire shift with her eyes closed tight, but suddenly moving forward seemed to take tremendous effort. It was as if the air had suddenly become heavy and she had to wade instead of walk.

Why did her entire being want to keep her from moving away from this man?

Because something in him drew her and the hold was stronger every time she was around him. She was a practical woman; she always prided herself on her good sense. Those traits seemed to have abandoned her now. One date and she was smitten. One kiss, and she'd hardly been able to focus on her day's work.

Brandilyn was in deep conversation with the Whitley family at table sixteen. She'd gotten their orders wrong. While the customers had been polite, Brandilyn burst into tears.

Paige laid her hand on the girl's shoulder, gave her a quick hug, and told her to take a much-needed break. By the time she'd sorted out what had gone wrong and how to fix it, and apologized profusely, several tables had finished and were heading up the aisle to queue up at the front counter to pay.

Instead of her mind being focused on asking Dave through the pass-through window to get a rush on the Whitleys' changes and hurrying to the till to ring up the sales, what was she doing?

Watching Evan. Noticing the way he sat so strong and straight. How those wide shoulders of his looked solid enough to carry any burden.

What should she do? He was a dream, and she didn't have time to dream.

## Chapter Thirteen

The next time Paige was able to catch a breath, she noticed Evan's chair was empty. Brianna was bussing his plate. The rush had hit, she'd been caught in the back, and now, an hour later as the dinner crowd was thinning, he was gone. And she hadn't gotten the chance to say goodbye.

"He left about five minutes ago." Dave gave a New York strip a flip on the grill and sprinkled seasoning across it. "Seemed to be looking around, like he was trying to find you to say goodbye. But that's when the twins' stepdad came to the back door and you went outside with him. Don't worry, Evan'll be back tomorrow."

"He'll be back as a customer."

"As a customer only? Nah, no customer looks at you the way he does."

"And what way would that be? As someone too busy to talk to him?"

"Nope." Dave grabbed a baked potato from the warmer. "As a man who's serious."

*Serious.* There was that word again. She'd never felt she had much in common with Cinderella before, but that's what this reminded her of. Last night's outing had been wonderful but it was way out of the ordinary. She was no beauty to make a man fall in love with her. She was no princess. Paige McKaslin had lines on her face, and gray hair she had her hairdresser color, and more responsibility than she would ever have free time.

Last night she'd put her bookkeeping aside to go out with him, thinking she could do it when she came home, and then the twins had landed on her doorstep. The girls had been in tears most of the night, distraught over their stepfather's drunken behavior and his terrible fight with their mother.

Tonight looked to be filled with even more drama and upset for the girls. And now the bookwork needed urgent attention.

Everything needed urgent attention.

The door swung open, jingling the welcome bell overhead. Paige automatically put a smile on her face, ready to greet whoever had stepped into her family's diner, and saw with relief that it was Alex and his girlfriend. She'd had a good talk with Beth before the lunch rush and had seen some real character in her. She was willing to work hard, and her reference from Misty at the drive-in was stellar.

"Thank you for hiring me, Mrs. McKaslin." Beth's thick hair was tied back at her nape and she'd come in comfortable shoes. "Here's the paperwork that you wanted, all filled out."

"You'll have to call me Paige, since you're working for me. Go ahead and put your things in back. Alex will show you where. Grab a bin and we'll start with bussing."

The teenagers headed off into the back, and Dave had an order up. Paige served the Monday meatloaf special and a cheeseburger to the young married couple she recognized as being new to the area, and hurried to tell the twins they should head on home—to her house. They were emotionally distraught, they'd gotten enough hours in to meet their income needs, and, as she reminded them, they'd had little sleep last night. A little relaxation was in order.

The twins seemed grateful about that, and Paige hugged each girl between ringing up the Redmonds' dinner, and sent them on their way. She kept an eye on Beth, who looked well practiced at bussing, while she whipped up a milkshake for Alex to nourish him while he studied at a table in back.

Already exhausted, she kept going, relieving Dave at the end of his shift. Taking calls for to-go orders, a follow-up call from Phil, who had put the estimate for the plumbing repairs in the day's mail for delivery tomorrow, and a frantic call to her CPA at his home, explaining the taxes were going to be, again, a last-minute thing. Good thing he was an understanding sort.

Then there were the bills to gather up to take home, orders to serve, customers to look after, especially old Mr. Corey who'd come in, alone and confused, to meet his wife for sundaes.

Paige sat him down to wait for his Rosie, who'd been buried eight years before, asked Beth not to let him out of her sight, and called his daughter. Shirley was frantic; her dad had wandered out of the house again. Dementia was a cruel enemy, and Paige sat with Mr. Corey trying to comfort him as he became more upset and saddened worrying over why his wife was late, until Shirley and her husband arrived to gently guide him home.

"That's so sad," Beth commented as the door swished shut behind the family.

"It is. There's a list of phone numbers tacked to the wall next to the register. Shirley's number is on it. Just so you know what to do."

Paige then seated the Everlys, who were out with their new baby girl. Family, she thought, was not only everything, it was the only thing. She'd taken care of her family for so long, and what would she do when they no longer needed her? She was losing them.

Her son was growing up. Her sister Rachel was now married and living in Florida, with a Special Forces husband and a stepdaughter she was close to. Amy was married and happy, and it was Heath's job to take care of her now. And her brother? Soldier Ben had finally married his high-school sweetheart and was currently serving in the Middle East.

One day Alex would be like this couple, she thought, as she took their beverage orders and took time to admire their newborn wistfully. Alex would be a strong, good man with a wife and family of his own.

All things change, but somehow the passing of time came bitterly. Maybe it was the punch of sadness over seeing poor Mr. Corey, who could not find his dear wife, and who had spent the last three years, as his mind deteriorated, looking for her always.

While she was sorry for Mr. Corey's condition, she couldn't help thinking what a great love he must have known. Real love. She believed in it.

She wasn't so sure if she believed it was possible for her. Or was it?

It was such a risk. Relationships failed all the time. Her gaze strayed to the chair where Evan usually sat in the evenings, occupied now by a couple of junior-high girls downing milkshakes and giggling.

When she was near to him, it seemed easier somehow to believe—just a little. The day was brighter, the shadows gentler with him nearby.

But now, as the night deepened and the demands of life remained, she didn't know how if she could possibly find the heart—or the faith—to really believe.

Evan pulled his truck to a stop in front of Paige's ranch house and killed the headlights. The night shadows were so thick, he could see nothing except for the thin line of lamplight between the seams of one of the large picture windows.

He imagined her sitting behind those curtains with her hair falling loose around her face as she bent over her bookkeeping.

His chest cinched up tight. Yep, he definitely had it bad. Whether he wanted to or not. Whether he was ready or not. He cared for the woman. So much for going slow and careful.

He opened the door, and his movements echoed in the stillness around him. He shut the truck door, careful not to spill the contents of the large grocery sack he carried. The night air was chilly, but the pungent aromas of greening grass and rising sap scented the darkness. The change of seasons rustled in the limbs overhead like a promise.

Paige. He could see her through the crack in the curtains. She sat at the kitchen table with paperwork spread out all around her feeding numbers into an adding machine. Her head was bent to her task with her dark hair spilling over her shoulders and hiding most of her face. Those dark rich strands shone like burnished silk in the lamplight, and he'd never seen anything more beautiful than this woman. His spirit stilled.

*She's the one.* He felt the truth deep in his soul. She'd brought him back to life.

He rapped lightly on the door. He could see her look up from her work and squint in his direction. Their gazes met. He felt her intake of breath and watched her eyes widen in surprise and then pleasure. Her smile was enough to jump-start his heart. She pushed away from the table, rising in her graceful, confident way and disappeared from his sight.

When the door opened, it was all he could do not to draw her into his arms and never let go. "Surprise. Someone has had a long work day."

"Longer than most, not that I'm complaining." She swept a shock of lustrous hair out of her eyes and stepped back, as if to welcome him in.

He stepped into the warmth and the light. "I've come to interrupt you."

"Good. I'm trying to come down with a headache."

"Accounting will do that. There is a remedy."

"I'm afraid to ask."

"Lead me to your kitchen and I'll show you."

"I'm not sure I should let you into my house. Maybe you should turn around and go back where you came from."

His eyes laughed at her as he closed the door. "Smart woman. But if you don't let me in, you'll never know what you missed."

"Oh, I'm not falling for that. I'm perfectly aware of what you want."

"I came to collect on my rain check. Remember?"

Oh, she remembered, all right. He'd wanted a hello kiss at the diner right in the middle of the dinner rush. "I don't seem to recall that kisses were offered on the menu."

"Something so rare and fine wouldn't be."

It was a sweet thing, how he came to her. Her heart fluttered with longing. It seemed unbelievable that he was here, that his warm hand was twining with hers, but this moment was real in a day that hadn't been the best.

Every heartache, every trouble, every worry eased as he brushed his lips across hers. And then there was only the silence of her soul, and a single moment of perfection.

When he moved away, it was as if he took a piece of her heart with him.

She was falling for him, and if she wasn't careful, she was going to fall so hard, she would never be able to get up again. What if this didn't work out? True love took time. Strong relationships took work. She couldn't go rushing into something she couldn't trust.

It was smarter to take a step back. "Now that you're here, can I get you something? I have hot tea."

He set the bag on the entryway table and stepped behind her. "Tea is fine, but let's get something straight. You will not wait on me."

"I won't?"

His hands settled onto her tense shoulders and began to knead at the knots there. "Did you stop long enough to eat supper?"

"I've been busy. I'm shorthanded down at the diner—"

"I bet you're always shorthanded at the diner. That's no excuse not to take care of yourself." His fingers dug into the sore flesh around her vertebrae.

*I could stand here forever.* She let her eyes drift shut. She hadn't realized her neck muscles were so tight. Stress, that's what it was. She knew she needed to slow down, but there would be time for that later. She had to get the diner in good enough shape to sell it. And once the business was off her shoulders, then she could take time.

But until then, all she could see was full steam ahead. It was as simple as that. As wonderful as Evan's neck massage was, she told herself that she didn't have time for closeness.

Or maybe, a small truthful voice said inside her, it was safer to step away.

"Did you want to come into the kitchen?" She took a step, twisting to break his hold, but his grip was like iron.

"I want you to take five minutes off." His words tingled against her ear. "I'll stay and help you for five minutes to make up for time lost."

"What do you know about bookeeping, exactly?"

"Uh, nothing. But what I lack in knowledge, I make up for in the willingness to work." His fingers stilled, and his hand settled against the curve of her neck, a heavy, possessive touch.

It was nice. It took every ounce of willpower she owned not to lean into him. Not to move closer. It was what she wanted so much. "Tea. I'll pour some tea. What's in the sack?"

He grabbed it with his free hand as he steered her toward the kitchen archway. "I noticed when I was at the diner that you were pretty busy. It's my guess that you work all evening serving other people their meals and never take the time to get dinner for yourself."

Good guess. But was she going to admit that? No! "I've been taking care of myself for a long time. I eat when I'm hungry. And when I can fit it in."

"Not good enough." Evan set his grocery bag on the counter and released his hold on her.

She stepped away with an odd sense of disconnection. Distance was what she wanted, but as she handed down two cups from the overhead cabinet, her heart wasn't so sure. She had to take down the tall walls she'd built so thick and sturdy that she would be safe from every harm.

Well, not *every* one. Evan. There he was in the edge of her peripheral vision, pulling covered plates from inside the paper sack. His powerful masculinity shrinking the large kitchen until he was all she could see. Every breath felt squeezed into her too-tight chest. She didn't want to feel this way. She couldn't help feeling this way.

He moved behind her and took the cups from her, his touch like warm steel against her. His voice was an intimate hush against her ear. "Take five minutes off. I meant it. Now go sit."

"I *am* taking five minutes off. You don't see me working do you?"

"This is what you do all day. Go to the table and let me do this for you. Please."

She twisted around to get a better look at him, and the affection she saw on his handsome face made something melt inside her. She was afraid it was a section of her defensive walls, and that just couldn't be good. "This is my kitchen. I don't take orders from men here."

"There's a first for everything." Humor tugged at

his mouth as he leaned to brush a kiss to her forehead.

Sheer tenderness. It flowed from him and into her heart like the rising of a tide.

"You like honey and cream, right?"

She blinked up at him, her mind strangely blank. Oh, in her tea. "Uh, yes."

Call her stunned, but he was actually working around her. He poured the tea and then opened the fridge for the small container of half-and-half. Her taxes were calling her, but for some reason she didn't care so much about the work needing to be done as about the man moving around her kitchen. See why it was a bad idea to let a man into her life?

Her senses honed to his every movement in her kitchen. She heard the rasp of the utensil drawer being opened. She couldn't remember the last time someone had served her something to eat.

He removed foil from the plates he'd brought. "Is Alex ready for graduation?"

Somehow she found her voice. "He's ready. I'm not. It's a good thing I'm so busy. That way I can't think too much about what it's going to be like when he's gone."

"Believe me, you'll have plenty of time once he is."

"That's what I'm afraid of." Her confession felt as dark as the night shadows, and she wished she could take back the words.

Evan turned, as if to come to her in comfort. Too overwhelmed, she slipped into the shadows on the other side of the counter. He studied her for a minute before going back to his work. "That's why I care about you so much, Paige. You deeply love your family and the people in your life."

She recognized the shadowed pain in his eyes, because it was so much like her own. "I guess we both know how important that is."

"It's everything." He slid two cups of tea across the counter. He said nothing more as he turned to fetch the plates he'd brought.

Paige took one look at the roast beef sandwiches on thick wheat bread and her jaw dropped. He was busy at the microwave and when she leaned across the bar chairs to hit the switch for the overhead track lighting, she caught the aroma of split pea soup. Sure enough, when the machine dinged, he withdrew a bowl of the thick, fragrant soup and fished through the drawers for a spoon.

When he returned, he swung into the bar chair across from her. "Is there anything else I can get you?"

"You could get me a time machine so I could propel myself into the future." She reached for the nearby paper-towel roll and ripped off two sheets.

He took the paper towel she offered. "Sorry, I left my time machine at home."

She folded her paper towel and laid it in her lap. "Maybe after the meal we could go over to your place so I could borrow it?"

"Why do you want to go back in time?"

"If I could, then I'd have my books done and I could put my feet up and not move for the rest of the evening." She bowed her head and said grace before she dipped her spoon into the hearty soup. "This is really good, Evan. Did you make it?"

"My grandmother's recipe. I have a few secret recipes in my family, too." He'd only made a half sandwich for himself, and he bit into a corner of it.

"This hits the spot. I hadn't realized how hungry I was. Thank you for being so thoughtful."

"I aim to please. It's the least I could do for all the times you've brought me a meal."

"That was at my restaurant and you were a paying customer."

"Well, I appreciate it." He grinned, emphasizing the dimples that dug into his lean cheeks.

His jaw had darkened with a five o'clock shadow, and Paige fought the urge to lay her fingertips there and feel that wonderful, manly texture. There were so many things she wanted to know about him. He obviously cooked. Did he like cooking? What did he do with his evenings? She wanted to know everything about him.

"If I really did have a time machine, I don't think

I would use it." Thoughtful, Evan stirred more sugar into his cup of tea.

"There's nothing you wouldn't change in your life?"

"No. I *should* want to go back to college and instead of proposing to Liz, I would break up with her. That would have saved me major heartache. But if I hadn't made the choice to marry her, then I never would have had my boys. Having them to raise was worth anything."

There was no mistaking Evan's love, and Paige understood what he meant. Romantic love had brought her nothing but pain in the end, but it had also given her Alex. "My son is my world. Even when he moves away, I'll have had eighteen years with him. The best years I have ever known."

"The years ahead will be as good. Different, but good, too."

Emotion clawed to life in her chest, and she grabbed her tea, hoping the soothing hot liquid would calm them. But no such luck. She drained the cup, fighting down something she couldn't name that felt surprisingly like panic. She needed the seventeen-year-old pain that still darkened her heart to have never existed. And how was that possible? She wouldn't have the best blessing in her life without her greatest heartbreak.

"Let me refill that for you." Evan was up and taking off with her cup before she could think to stop him.

Now there's a change. She remembered Jimmy and how he'd never thought a man's place was in the kitchen. Oddly enough, he was the day-shift cook at the diner but when he came home, he expected to be the king of his castle. And that meant she was the maid, the cook and everything else. It was strange to see a man looking at home in her kitchen, as if pouring tea and stirring sugar and cream into the cup was no big deal.

He set the cup into its saucer with an easy smile. "Why do you look so sad?"

"Oh, it's because I don't like bookkeeping. It bums me out and that makes me remember things best left forgotten."

"I had a lot of those things, too. Things that are better off buried from the light of day." He returned to the bar chair beside her, moving slowly, as if he felt her sadness. "I would never have come here and brought you a meal if I knew it reminded you of your ex."

She closed her eyes against the past and the pain. It was over and done with; she'd let the wounds heal and went on with the demands of her life. "You don't remind me of Jimmy at all. He never would have brought me a cup of tea, let alone made sure I had supper after a long day on my feet."

"What on earth could be more important to a man than his wife?"

How could he be real? He had to be a figment of her imagination. A piece of fiction projected like a movie in front of her. He said the right things. He did the right things. He was everything he was supposed to be, but she'd believed in a man once who had seemed so strong. Who had seemed like everything she'd ever prayed for in a man.

And now she had no excuses. No man had ever measured up to her ideal, and she believed that no man ever would. So that made it easy. She didn't have to risk. She didn't have to trust. She didn't have to put the most vulnerable parts of herself on the line.

She didn't know if she ever could.

"It was nice that you came over. And this meal. This is the nicest thing a man's done for me. Really. Evan, I truly like you, but I don't have time for this. For dating and as much as I want—" Oh, she couldn't finish that one. Time to think before you speak, Paige, or you'll be spilling your heart to this man. Evan was a good man, but he was still a man. She couldn't allow herself to look at him and see eternity. She leaped to her feet in panic. "I've got to get back to work. Let me rinse off your plates."

"Leave it." He sounded harsh. He stared up at her as if thunderstruck.

She'd hurt him. She didn't want to hurt him. "It's

not you, Evan. I just—" She couldn't finish the sentence or the thought. What she wanted rang in her heart. *I want you.* But what she wanted was a good, decent, unfailing man. And few men were like that.

In a flash, her mind leaped back in time. She shook as images of late-night fights flashed through her mind. Wee hours of the night when she'd been too exhausted and stressed and miserable. When she'd managed to get the baby back to sleep—*again*—and Jimmy still wasn't home.

Worse images of what had happened when he did come home, drunk and in a mood. He would start in on her, yelling and criticizing, angry that everyone and everything else was more important to her than he was.

"I'm just trying to pay the bills, Jimmy," she'd tell him. "We need to pull together, not apart." But there was always something that kept their world off kilter: Ben being dragged in by the local sheriff, Amy suspended from school, the baby was colicky again and the endless demands of the diner. It *was* all work and no play. But that was life, right?

It was not the life Jimmy wanted. Paige knew she was a decent and hard-working woman, but she wasn't enough. She wasn't prettier, more interesting, and, as time proved, she wasn't enough to love. He'd gone outside their marriage, he'd cheated, and he'd had fun, as he told her on their last day as man and wife. His parting words replayed in her mind as they had a thousand times since that heartbreaking night. "The only special thing about you is that you can work. You're useful, but what man would really love you?"

She was terrified that if she risked so much of her heart on Evan, one day he would finally get to know the real her.

And think the same thing.

So, what did she say to Evan? He'd come here with his caring and his heart and his thoughtful meal. She wanted...it didn't matter what she wanted. She swiped the bowl beneath warm water and scrubbed it with the pre-soaped scrubber she kept on the back of the sink. The running water drowned out the sound of him moving toward her. The wild thumping of her heart drowned out the sound of him moving away from her.

When she shut off the water, he wasn't at the door. He was putting her untouched sandwich on a plate he'd found in the cupboard and wrapping it in cellophane. His movements were deliberate and confident. "I'll leave this for later. You may get hungry after you're done figuring out your books."

"Or need consolation only good food can provide."

With a nod, he placed the wrapped plate into her refrigerator. The dependable line of his shoulders and the straight plane of his back blurred as she dried his bowl and handed it to him.

"Th-thanks." The words came out stilted and resonating pain. She winced. She didn't want him to know that his kindness was hurting her. Because he was the wished-for dream she'd stopped believing in long ago.

He placed the bowl with his plates into the grocery sack and rolled down the top. "When I give my word, I mean it. When I give my heart, I give it completely. And just so you know, I don't scare off easily. Good night, pretty lady."

With a lopsided grin that was at once both serious and charming, he walked out of her house and into the night.

## Chapter Fourteen

The shrill ring of her bedside phone woke Paige out of a dreamless sleep. Confused, she groped in the dark for the phone. Her hand hit something hard—not the phone, she realized too late as it hit the floor. Probably her devotional.

The receiver rang again and she snatched it up, her thoughts coming at the speed of light. Alex was downstairs asleep in his room. Amy and Heath had stayed home tonight. That meant something was wrong with Ben. He'd been shot in combat again? Her pulse fluttered with fear.

Or what if something had happened to Rachel's husband, who was also on active duty? "Hello?"

"Paige?" It was a man's voice she recognized, but she couldn't place it. She sat up in bed as he continued. "This is Cam Durango."

*The sheriff.* "What's wrong? What happened?" Her mind groped at the possibilities. Amy was pregnant. Had she been rushed to the hospital?

"It's the diner. I'm sorry to have to tell you this, but it's on fire. My deputy was driving by on patrol through town and saw the flames. He called the fire department and started in on fighting it—"

"I'll be right there." She slammed down the phone before she realized she hadn't let the sheriff finish. A thousand unasked questions zoomed through her mind. She was suddenly awake and moving too slowly. She couldn't seem to move fast enough. She pulled on last night's jeans and sweater.

"Mom?" Alex was bounding down the hall when she stumbled through her bedroom door. His hair stood up on end and his dog ran along at his side. "What's wrong? What can I do to help?"

"I need you to stay here. It's the diner. It's on fire. The sheriff said—" *It can't be on fire.* It seemed unreal to be shrugging into her jacket so she could drive to town and watch her diner burn. She wanted to offer up a prayer, but she didn't even know what to pray for.

"Mom? I'm driving you." Alex took her keys from the hook above the entry table. He'd already jabbed his bare feet into a pair of boots by the door. He grabbed the door and his coat at the same time.

His hand at her elbow felt steady and strong. Her

boy was turning into a fine young man. She let him lead her outside, leaving the dog behind to whine. It seemed just like a nightmare as she settled into the passenger seat of her SUV and waited to see smoke and flames.

She wasn't disappointed. As they rolled down the deserted street into town, she saw the smoke cloud blotting out the constellations. The acrid scent filtered into the vehicle as the black ribbon of the street led them to the strobe of sirens. A fire tanker from Bozeman was pulling in beside the city and county vehicles. Flames writhed like orange monsters, giving eerie flashes of illumination into the burning building.

This was no dream. She gripped the seat belt like an anchor. There was a horrible thundering sound and men's voices rose in alarm. A split second later, the roof crumbled into the ruins of the diner, and fire surged up into the night sky like rockets.

Tears blurred her vision as she watched the building that had been both burden and blessing burn into ember and ash.

Although her back was to him, Evan recognized Paige in an instant. Even with his eyes closed, he felt her nearness in the deepest places of his heart, as if she were the reason it beat. He pocketed his truck keys and hurried down the sidewalk, past the grocery and across the street to where she stood at the barrier a few yards from the fire trucks.

She looked defeated, Evan thought as he hopped out of the truck and onto the blacktopped street. She looked beaten, and he hurt for her. With her. He hated how her head bowed forward and her shoulders drooped as if she'd lost her best friend. He knew what that diner meant to her, her great responsibility to her family, and as the building rubble burned, he knew she felt as if she'd failed them. He knew because he could feel the heaviness of her emotions in his chest. He felt the black void inside her as if it were inside himself.

*I love her.* The simple fact didn't amaze him. He knew the fall had been inevitable. It had only been a question of when. As he crossed the last yard of distance that separated him from her, he had to hold back the fierce need to make her world right. It was all he wanted to do for the rest of his life.

The last steps he took toward her were certain. Unwavering. He laid his hand on her nape. "How can I help you?"

The muscles beneath his touch tensed even more, but she didn't jump. As he thought, she'd sensed his approach. "What about that time machine? I could really use that right now—"

There was no mistaking the anguish reflecting darkly in her eyes. Before he could answer, her sister did. Amy stood huddled against her husband's side, her face streaked with tears. "This isn't your fault, Paige. Stop second-guessing yourself."

"I don't remember if I double-checked my night list. I had a lot on my mind. I could have left the fryers on. I could have—"

"You never forget anything. Stop torturing yourself. Please."

Paige's tension surged through Evan as she turned to face him. Soot streaked her beautiful face. "Evan, it's two-thirty in the morning. You should be home in bed. Why? Why are you here?"

"I got a call from your son."

"Alex? What was he doing calling you? I sent him home. It's too bad he's not still here, or I'd make him apologize for disturbing you—"

"Disturbing me? No! I'm here because I care about you." *Because I love you,* he wanted to say but he wasn't ready. But he already knew he *was* ready to be the man who stood beside her through this. The man who was never going to let her down. "I've told you before. I'm not the kind of man who bails. So what if it is two-thirty in the morning? I'm tough. I can handle it."

Evan's hand settled against the small of her back, a steely comfort so wonderful, she was afraid to accept it for fear that comfort would vanish. She didn't want to feel that harsh sting of disappointment when she found out Evan was just a man, after all, used to taking and not giving.

Not every man is like that, Paige, you know that.

She did; but the heart had no logic and fear had a life of its own. She stepped up to the barrier, trying to trust the steady pressure of Evan's hand on her spine and his iron presence at her side as he followed her.

Some of the firemen were leaving. The Bozeman department began to roll up their hoses. The flames were gone, and only the glowing embers within the black rubble seemed to be left to deal with. The local department appeared very busy. The wind changed direction, and the acrid-scented air thickened.

"I'm glad you're here, Thornton." Heath, Amy's husband, met his gaze over his wife's head. "I want to gct Amy home, but Paige  "

Evan nodded, and a moment of understanding passed between them. Paige was a strong woman, but she was also vulnerable. She needed care. And he was the man to do it.

After the sisters said goodbye and embraced, he watched in silence as Paige turned away from him. She wrapped her arms around her waist, as if she had no one else to hold on to. "You should go home, Evan. It was good of you to come, but there's nothing you can do. There's nothing anyone can do at this point."

"No, the fire can't be undone."

"Some things are so devastating, the damage can never be undone." She sounded hollow.

He knew she had to be in shock. To her, the diner wasn't only a building made of wood and drywall, he knew, it meant so much more. It represented an important part of her past. Her parents had run the place. It was also her future. She had to have been counting on it as her livelihood for the years to come.

He could feel the pain rolling through him as if their hearts were connected. This was something he'd never felt before. Something he'd heard about from Phil and Marie and some of his friends at the office, a special God-given connection that was rare and wondrous.

Love in all its forms was a blessing, but this, he realized, was extra special. Like a piece of heaven brought to earth just for the two of them.

Her hands were ice when he cupped them. "You're not alone, Paige. Remember that."

"I can't even think about what this means. The twins. They need the job to stay in school. And Jodi, my morning waitress? She's been with me since we both were in high school. What's she going to do?" She wrenched her hands from his and covered her eyes. She wasn't crying, but the agony reflected in the tight line of her jaw said everything.

He tried to imagine the woman he'd been married

to caring so much about other people, but it was difficult, for she'd been so concerned in looking out for her own interests that she'd even neglected their sons. But Paige was the exact opposite. She was giving and loyal and strong. She was everything he admired and respected in a woman.

If he made a list and wrote down on a sheet of paper every trait he'd hoped for in a wife, the kind he could trust with his life and his heart, she would meet every criterion. But being with a woman in a long-term relationship was about more than admiring her good traits. Much, much more.

And that emotion sang through him, like a hymn coming to life in a quiet sanctuary. Love. The real kind that filled a man up and wasn't whole until it was given away. Rare, pure tenderness swelled in his soul until he couldn't breathe, until he couldn't think, until all he could see was Paige. Paige, who was hurting. He wanted to ease her pain. He wasn't going to let her stand alone. Not tonight. Not for the rest of her life.

"Evan. Paige." It was Cameron Durango, the town sheriff and captain of the volunteer fire crew. He swiped the soot from his face as he approached the temporary barrier. "We've got the fire out. It's a total loss, as you can see. I am sorry."

"Do you know what started it?" Her voice trembled as if she were afraid of the answer.

Evan curled his fingers around hers. She needed him, and he would be here for her, now and always.

Cameron shook his head. "Not until the county fire marshal comes to take a look at it. I'll tell you this, though, it didn't start in the kitchen. The worst damage is in the wall by the electrical panel. My best guess is that a short in a wire started this. I'll be in touch tomorrow. You might as well take her home, Evan."

"No, I want to stay—" Paige began.

Evan tightened his hold on her. "Cameron's right. There's nothing you can do, baby. Not until the ruins cool down."

"The ruins. My diner is in ruins."

He wanted to protect her; he wanted to take care of her. He wanted her in the most fundamental ways and the most emotional. "Thanks, Cam. I'll take her home."

As the fireman moved away, Evan pulled his beloved to his chest and held her. She was trembling, as if from more than the chill night. As if from more than fear at the uncertain turn her life had taken. When the right time came, he would reassure her. He wasn't going anywhere; he'd stand by her. He would move heaven and earth if he had to, if only to make sure she was well and secure.

As he led her to his truck, his grip was constant devotion that kept her from stumbling when she tripped. He opened the passenger door, and the dome light spilled over her like a blessing. She was a light that hurt his eyes to see, and yet he could not look away. He took a ragged breath, finally squeezing air into his lungs. What did a man do when he was struck so hard? When love rendered him powerless?

When heaven was within his reach right here on earth?

A man stood tall, that's what he did, to protect and preserve this rare gift. Tenderly, he helped Paige into the truck and pulled the seat belt for her. She looked too dazed and exhausted to do more than offer a quiet thanks.

"Any time, gorgeous." That made her smile, if only a watery weak one, but it was enough.

He could feel the change in his spirit like calmness coming to this turbulent night. Committed love filled him, slow and steady, and he knew, from this moment on, his life would be devoted to her, come what may.

Paige covered her face with her hands and closed her gritty, burning eyes. The truck bounced along the ruts at the end of her driveway and eased to a stop in front of her house. Alex had left the porch light on, which broke the endless blackness of the night, and she gave thanks for her fine son, who was already such a reliable young man. He'd been wonderful tonight, taking charge and taking care. He'd called the rest of the family. His only mistake was in calling Evan Thornton.

What was she going to do about Evan? She glanced at him out of the corner of her eyes as he killed the engine and switched off the headlights. He sat straight and tall behind the wheel, moving with a masculine confidence as he unbuckled his seat belt and reached for her hand. His touch was as warm as comfort, and there was something awesome about him, and it broke her heart.

She wished she *could* rely on a man, one who would never let her down again. Evan was a steadfast man. She admired him. She respected the man she'd come to know, but the future was an uncertain place.

And trusting a man enough to really love him, trusting him enough to let real, true love happen, was a complete risk.

*Don't do it!* every instinct within her warned as she opened the door and climbed out into the cool night. She shivered, but not from the wind. She felt broken, as if something within her had crumbled to ashes right along with the diner.

It took her a moment to register that Evan's steps sounded behind hers on the concrete walkway. "Go home. It's late. You have work tomorrow."

"No way. I'm not going anywhere until I know you're all right."

Please, don't be wonderful to me. It would make

it too hard to resist placing her trust in him completely, and she couldn't do that. She felt battered and lost and vulnerable enough that she would reach right out to him and let him into her heart. And she couldn't do that. She couldn't risk that.

As she opened the door, she blinked against the blinding light and wondered where her defenses had gone. The iron willpower she'd used to stand on her own two feet for seventeen long years seemed to have crumbled.

For the first time since Jimmy had walked out on her, she felt as if she were falling through thin air, sure of certain impact. If she reached out to stop her fall, it would be Evan she grabbed. Evan, so good and dependable, and she didn't want to need him. She couldn't let herself really need him. Why did she think she ever could?

"Here. Let me take your coat." He was calm and in control, and it felt just right to be so close to him that she could rest her cheek against his chest if she wanted to. His fingertips scraped the nape of her neck as he helped her out of her sooty jacket and hung it over the closet doorknob.

She was too dazed to do more than turn toward the kitchen. She didn't know what to do. How was it that everything around her was exactly as it always was, when something so catastrophic had happened? It didn't make any sense.

Evan's hand gripped the curve of her shoulder. "Come sit down. Let me make you some tea."

She moved woodenly, hardly aware of making her way to the small round table in the shadowed nook. The table where her taxes sat in a pile. Was it just a few hours ago she'd been here with Evan? How could everything seem so normal, when so much had changed?

"All settled?" Evan towered above her, haloed by the glare of the light slanting in from the entry and, cast in silhouette, he seemed to radiate more might, if that were possible.

This man had come to her in the middle of the night. He'd stood at her side and never wavered. He'd comforted her, helped her at every chance, and was, at 4:10 in the morning in the process of nuking her a cup of water.

Don't get too used to it, a small voice inside her whispered. It was neither a wise voice nor a kind one, but, she feared, it was a sensible one.

She'd learned before that men could be one way and then, over time, or when their reasons were different, they could let you fall to the ground faster than you could see coming.

Evan's not like that, she argued, managing what she hoped passed for a smile as he slid a steaming mug with a floating tea bag onto the table in front of her.

"Thanks. You've been pretty wonderful tonight."

"Yeah? I'm glad you think so. This is only the start, Paige. Just the beginning."

Oh, how she wanted to believe him completely. To grab tight to his words, and to him, as if she could keep this moment, when he stood over her so tall and invincible and committed, and make it last forever.

The deepest places in her *wanted* to believe.

"Want honey and cream?" His rough, intimate baritone made her soul shiver.

"Uh, n-no." She hardly tasted the sweet soothing warmth of the chamomile. Her senses seemed to freeze. And then empty.

And fill with him. Evan's voice. Evan's deep bronze-flecked eyes. Evan's warm, male-textured hand covering hers as he knelt at her side. He overwhelmed her. He filled her. He made it impossible to push him away, impossible to pretend she didn't need anyone, especially him.

Her throat ached with the knot of emotions, wanting to need him and being afraid to, so that she couldn't speak, only nod, in answer. The tea was fine. The tea wasn't the problem.

The problem was the man who was as true as could be. She'd never had a man stay beside her as if a tornado couldn't unseat him.

Or a man with such a heart. A man she could love with every bit of her soul.

"I'm sorry about your diner. It's a terrible loss. I know it's how you make your living. Whatever you need, I'm right here for you. Money. Moral support. Prayer. More tea."

Oh, I could so love this man. The enormity of it terrified her. "I have to deal with the insurance people. I have to—"

"Don't worry about that now. You're not alone with this, baby. You're not alone any more."

She felt as if she were plunging through thin air, falling fast and hard toward the canyon floor below. She feared that when she hit, the impact would blow her apart. It felt as if her life was already in pieces. She didn't feel as if she could take another heartbreak.

She'd thought she could try to find love with this wonderful man. But she'd only been kidding herself with falsehoods.

The truth was that men left, and she wanted to push him away and take out on him the pain she knew he would bring her one day. The same pain Jimmy had given her when he'd told her she wasn't enough for him, or for any man.

But that wasn't the truth at all. She scrubbed at her eyes, burning and gritty from the smoke. Be honest, Paige, she ordered herself. Not all men left women. There were plenty of good decent men who stayed with their wives, who stuck with their families through thick and thin.

The truth was, men left *her*. She felt the night's shadows creep into the empty places in her soul. In places that had been hurting for too long. What if she *wasn't* enough? She wasn't worldly or gorgeous or exciting and never would be. Doubts were like a small crack in a bone that grew and grew until the sting of it had her eyes watering. She loved him completely, this man who had stolen every last piece of her heart. What was she going to do when he turned away from her? When he said to her that she wasn't fun enough or exciting enough to love?

She'd lost a major part of her heart when Jimmy headed for the door. If Evan left her, what would he take with him? A part of her very soul? That's how much she loved him now. What about in time, as she came to love him more? What would she do if he left her to fall? What would she do on the day to come when he no longer cared if he hurt her or not?

*I can't go through that again, Lord.* She swiped at her tears, but they came too fast and too hot and she couldn't see as she put down the cup with a clink to the tabletop.

"Hey, it's going to be okay. I promise." He said those words with the greatest of convictions, as if he would move mountains stone by stone just for her. "Here, lean on me."

She wanted to. She ached to be weak, just for a

moment, and sink against his strength. To let him hold her up just for a bit. She wished she could rest her cheek against the invincible plane of his chest and feel his arms around her and simply hold on. Maybe then she wouldn't fall.

Who was she kidding? Leaning on a man was the greatest danger of all.

Terror filled her. If she could just give in. Just trust. Believe that he would hold on to her forever, come what may.

Surrender, Paige. She willed herself to lean toward him. His chest felt strong. His arms would hold her tight. He wouldn't fail her. He wouldn't move away. He wouldn't buckle and let her fall.

*I can't do it, Lord.* Terror clawed through her like a hunted animal trying to escape, and she turned away. "I need you to go. I just need—" She squeezed her eyes shut. She couldn't take seeing his strong arms or his iron-hard chest or the rejection in his eyes when she pushed him away.

Since it was inevitable, she covered her face with her hands. "Go home. Evan. Please."

"But you're not okay."

"S-sure I am." She bit her bottom lip to keep in the sob. "I'm free. That diner has been a weight around my neck for too long. Alex graduates in two weeks, and he'll be gone. I can finally do whatever I want. I'm free. That's my d-dream, you know."

Liar, she called herself. Evan was her real dream. And a dream was all it could ever be. Ever.

She couldn't trick herself into wishing for impossible dreams. Fairy tales were fiction, and so were the heroic men in them. This was real life. Evan, as good as he was, was an everyday, ordinary man. And she was too broken and scarred.

She'd lost her heart long ago and there wasn't enough left of her to try marriage again. "I'm sorry. I really am, t-to have d-dated you. And let you think—"

She couldn't go on. His jacket sleeve rustled when he lifted his arm. He was reaching out to pull her close. Panic blinded her. She bolted out of the chair. He gaped up at her with hurt blazing in his eyes, still kneeling, his arm frozen in midair.

*I've hurt him.* The impact rocked through her. She'd been afraid of being devastated and look at what she'd done. She'd drawn first blood.

*I want to love him more than anything.* She scrubbed the tears out of her eyes so she could see enough to walk away from him.

## Chapter Fifteen

For a moment, his faith in her wavered. She was finally free? She wanted freedom? This was news to him. Yet she'd talked about her son leaving. She'd talked about needing to fill the emptiness left behind by her son.

Maybe she's telling the truth, he thought, as pain crushed his heart. Maybe he was only someone to pass the time with until she was free of her responsibilities?

And then the shock of her words wore off. What she was saying didn't make sense. Paige hadn't dated once in the seventeen years since her husband ran out on her. She was nothing like Liz. He knew. Paige didn't use people, she didn't give excuses; she was his dream come true.

A dream he still believed in.

She held up her hands helplessly, tears streaming down her face. "I was wrong to let you think this c-could work between us. I didn't mean to h-hurt you. I really thought—"

"Why can't it work between us?" He was already on his feet and crossing the room. "Everything was all right until tonight. Until I was trying to hold you and I felt you tense up. I felt it, Paige, and I'll be—" He bit his bottom lip, determined not to curse. Frustration burned like an ulcer in his guts. His heart still felt as if it was being axed apart. He had to take a deep breath and try again. "I won't let this go. Do you understand? I love you."

"No, you don't love me."

"Don't tell me what I feel." He knew she'd had a terrible blow tonight, but didn't she know she was throwing away something that was real? When he opened his heart, she was there. Where she would be forever.

"Maybe it's my fault for not telling you sooner. But it isn't easy for a man like me. I've been alone for a long time, and I've gotten used to keeping my feelings below the surface. And you—" How did he tell her all that was in his heart? "You are the sweetest thing I've known. You make my day brighter. My life better. And me, you make me happy. I love you so much."

"You love me?"

"Why do you think I came to you tonight?"

"I don't know." If her brain would start working right again, then she might be able to tell him. She fought to take a normal breath and to dig beneath the panic threatening to swallow her in one great bite. "Alex called you. He told you about the fire."

"But I came because I wanted to be with you. To stand beside you. Because that's what a man does when he loves a woman more than his own life. He sticks by her. He's her rock when she needs strength. He's her soft place when she needs comfort—"

"No." His words hurt as if they were a thousand tiny arrows piercing her skin, drawing blood and digging deep. "Those are only words. Love isn't like that."

"Yes. Real love is."

"You can't make me believe—"

"That's going to be my job for the rest of my life." Incredibly, he cupped his warm palm against the curve of her face, breaching the distance between them. "To make you believe."

"I c-can't believe you." He was stealing every last bit of her heart and she couldn't stop him. Her feelings were out of her control; she couldn't stop the love bursting up through the shroud of doubt and fear, shining brighter than any light and more certain than any dawn. But she could not let go of her fears. "I can't go through that again. I just can't."

"It's an unconscionable thing, what people do to one another. He hurt you deeply. I know, because I've been hurt like that, too. *Hurt* is too small a word when the one person you love and trust beyond all else on this earth betrays you, and it cuts you down to the soul." Instead of moving away, instead of buckling like water beneath sand, he moved closer, a towering strength that did not yield.

"You're never the same when someone does that to you," she confessed.

"No. I'll never understand how some people can have everything that matters and not be happy with it. I'm not like that. I know how valuable you are. I see you, Paige, clear down to your soul, and loving and honoring you is a commitment I will make to you every single day to come. Because you are worth it."

No, a voice deep inside her cried, because it could not be true. *He* could not be true. She could not believe in dreams and flattery.

But this was Evan, stalwart, steadfast Evan, and his goodness was breaking her will. His love was breaking her heart.

The voice of her past, the one she'd internalized for so long, was Jimmy's voice. How did she silence it? How did she erase his damaging words from the broken places in her soul? *No one can love you,* he'd told her and she'd let those words in, and she'd believed them.

She didn't want to believe them anymore.

"I love you so very much, Paige McKaslin." He was honesty and faith and commitment, a dream that she could not believe in.

A dream that seemed too rare to be true. Too amazing to happen to her after being alone, and without romance, for so long. Love was a dangerous risk. There were no guarantees, and love demanded a person's everything—her vulnerability and her openness. Romance needed belief to have a chance. And she so wanted this to have a chance.

Terror filled her. But the power of it was nothing compared to the warmth that seemed to surround her like a glowing, iridescent cloud. A shimmering brightness of love that she could not deny, although it was felt and not seen, emotional and not tangible, but it was there all the same. Love, true and pure, in Evan's gaze, in Evan's words, and, once again, in his touch resolute against her cheek.

And then she knew. If she did not risk, she would hurt him. If she did not trust, she would break his heart. If she did not love him truly, then she would be turning her back on the precious, committed love he offered her. And she would rather die before she caused Evan the tiniest pain.

In the end, wasn't love like faith? They were both unseen, but felt. And both were more powerful than any force in the universe. And that force rose up from her soul.

As if Evan could feel the change within her, he leaned closer. Her pulse fluttered in anticipation. There was a man strong enough to stand beside her in this life, and that man was Evan.

His kiss was a warm certain brush against her lips. His tenderness unmistakable.

Yes, her heart knew for sure. *He is the one.*

Dazed, she opened her eyes and met his gaze full-force. Flat-out, nothing held back, all defenses down, she could not stop the sting of emotion rising up within her.

True unshakable love shone through her, chasing away every shadow in her soul.

This was her chance. God was giving her this man and his love and it was up to her. All she had to do was trust and take the biggest risk of her life.

"I love you, Evan Thornton. With all of my soul." *Thank you, Lord, for this woman.*

Evan gently tucked his beloved against his chest. Peace filled him. Holding her was like finding the missing part of himself. Like filling a place that had always been empty within him. Pressing a kiss to the crown of her head was tenderness and commitment and a dream all wrapped up in one unbelievable blessing. Tears wet his shirt as she pressed against him, leaning into him, holding on.

He ached with a love so pure, he could not begin to describe it to her. So he simply held his dear Paige, feeling their breathing slow and fall into rhythm together.

He couldn't stop the images that poured up from his soul. Images of marrying her in the old-fashioned church in town. Of making a home together. Of coming home to her every evening.

Their sons would be stepbrothers. There would be marriages one day, grandchildren…family.

And he would be happy, he knew, because he would spend each day to come with this woman, with his incredible Paige. Love burned like a supernova within him.

"This is forever," he vowed and kissed her sweet lips.

# Epilogue

*The Sunshine Café's Reopening Day, Late August.*

Paige pushed through the swinging doors into the brand-new kitchen. The sight of her sister Amy and her husband side by side at the grill brought a smile to her face and happiness to her whole heart. "Are you ready to take a break yet, Amy?"

"Are you kidding? I'm just getting started." She glowed in her fourth month of pregnancy, now that the tough stretch of morning sickness was past. "It looks like a full house from here."

"I'm going to open up the patio. Customers are still arriving." As she spoke, the bell on the front door jangled, announcing new arrivals. She swept four house salads onto her tray. Her two-caret emerald-cut diamond sparkled cheerfully in the generous sunlight from the windows, a constant reminder of Evan's love and faith.

Life is good, she thought as she drizzled dressing on the fresh greens. She would always be grateful for the blessing of Evan's love. She'd never been happier. She hefted the tray. "In ten more minutes, you take a break, sister dear. Or I'll come hunt you down and make you take one."

"Promises, promises."

The dining room was cheerful and full of light. Families gathered together, talking and laughing and enjoying their meals. The long row of garden windows on two sides of the building gave the diners lovely views of the park across the street and of the small woods at the side of the property. It had been the right decision to rebuild, she thought as she hustled down the wide aisle. Jodi, who'd been the morning waitress for nearly twenty years and was practically family, was now set to buy the place.

"Hey, Mom. Are you sure you don't want me to get up and help?" Alex, back from his summer as a camp counselor, looked so grown-up and suntanned, even she hardly recognized him.

He grinned at her from the sunny booth where he sat with Westin, Amy's son. They were playing a game of Battleship while devouring a platter of French fries.

Oh, it was good to have her boy back home again, even if it was for only a few days before she and Evan would be taking him to college. "Are you kidding? You just got home. Relax for a change."

Over the din of cheerful conversations, Paige hustled down the wide aisle. Brianna was seating the Brisbane family while her twin sister rang up the Whitley family's ticket at the front counter.

God is gracious, she thought as she served the Corey family their salads. The diner was beautiful, a new start for the building and the business, and although her life was going to take her in new directions, this place would always remind her of sweet memories. She'd grown up here, underfoot as her parents worked. Alex had grown up here, playing his electronic games in the corner or lost in a book while she ran the business.

Everything changed. That was life. And changing brought the sting of loss and the joy of new beginnings.

She promised the Corey family that their New York steaks would be coming soon. The front bell had her looking toward the door. A petite woman, slim and fashionable, stood in the light of the windows, looking too mature and confident to be her other little sister. A little girl with bountiful curls clutched her hand and gazed around wide-eyed.

Rachel! Paige was running, her heart wide open, her vision blurring. She had her sister in her arms and gave her a tight squeeze. "Oh, you're here. What are you doing here? I can't believe it! You look gorgeous!"

"I wanted to surprise you. Did I?" She stepped back, sun-browned and trim and happy.

Happy. Paige was so grateful for that. She'd worried so at first, when Rachel had met Jake, that he had ulterior motives for proposing marriage. But there was no mistaking Rachel's deep contentment. She'd known Rachel was happy and that her marriage was working well, because they talked on the phone every chance they got. But there was nothing like seeing in person that it was true. Rachel had found her happily ever after.

"Jake's on temporary duty in Afghanistan, but Sally and I decided to fly up and see the new place. Didn't we, baby?"

"Yep." Sally nodded, a little shy, and leaned against Rachel's hip, a clear sign the girl had finally come to trust and love her new stepmother. "I'm real hungry. For a chocolate milkshake?"

Ah, a little niece to spoil, Paige thought. What fun. "With lots of whipped cream on top and chocolate sprinkles? Did you want to go sit with Westin, sweetie?"

"Okay."

A squeal rang through the restaurant behind them. It was Amy, flying down the aisle to wrap Rachel into a sisterly hug. While they cried and chatted excitedly together, Paige took Sally to Alex's table with promises to return soon. "With Tater Tots?" the little girl asked, with the cutest grin.

"Hey, beautiful," a man's voice murmured against her ear as she slipped Sally's order to the wheel. "Whatcha doin' later?"

"I'm having dinner with my handsome fiancé."

"He's one lucky guy. Handsome huh?"

"Very." She turned in his arms, feeling the quiet rush of joy brimming her soul. Her dear Evan. He was her forever love. Her hero of a man. She ran her fingertips against the roughness of his jaw. Because of this good man, she knew what love really was. It was like the mountains she could see from the window, majestic and unfailing. Her life was better because of him. She was better because of him.

He took her left hand and dropped a tender kiss to her engagement ring. "How's the new engagement ring feel?"

"Like a dream come true. I can't believe I get to be your wife."

"Are you kidding? I get to be your husband. December can't come fast enough." Evan wanted to be married to her now, but they were going to wait until all the family could be together. The boys would be home from school. Her brother would be back from active duty in the Middle East. His parents were planning to drive up from their retirement home in Scottsdale.

It was right that they say their vows before the witnesses who mattered the most, because this was it. It was forever. A once in a lifetime love that he wanted to celebrate not just on their wedding day, but for every day to come. She wasn't just the kind of woman he'd never thought he would find, but she was more wonderful than he ever could have imagined. Where once his life had been steady and predictable and his future a long vast stretch of emptiness, now there was her. And she was everything.

He brushed the hair from her eyes, so he could better look into their dazzling depths. Forever with her would not be long enough. "I know you're busy, but we have reservations for six o'clock."

"Jodi promised she'd take over at six."

"That's in five minutes from now."

"I know. Don't worry. I wouldn't miss time with you for anything." She brushed a kiss to his lips. "There's Cal now. I see him driving up. You two go get settled, and I'll be right out. The Coreys' steaks are up."

Evan. He was her life now. Paige finished her

shift by serving the Coreys and made sure they had everything they needed, steak sauce and extra sour cream and refills on their drinks. Then she untied her apron, hung it in the office, and left the responsibility of the dinner rush in Jodi's capable hands.

Her family was waiting for her. Beth, who was off tonight, had wedged into the booth at Alex's side. They were busy talking across the table to Cal, who sat next to his father. A table had been pulled up to the corner booth, to make enough room for Rachel, who was still talking with Amy. Westin and Sally were beginning a game of Battleship.

"Right here, baby." Evan had kept a spot for her at his side and he held out his hand, tender as he'd always been and would always be.

She settled at his side, where she would be for the rest of her life. The front bell chimed again, and it was Blake, Evan's first son, sauntering through the doorway. He waved when he spotted them.

So much in her life was changing. Her son was a man now. The diner would be Jodi's to run. Her sisters were married and happy. Next month she would start her first two classes at MSU in Bozeman, a thirty-nine-year-old freshman who was planning a Christmas wedding. Finally, she had her fairy-tale ending. Her happily ever after.

And all because of the man who leaned close to

kiss her cheek. She shivered down to the bottom of her soul. This was simply another beginning.

The best one of all.

\* \* \* \* \*

Dear Reader,

Thank you for choosing *A Handful of Heaven*. I hope you enjoyed reading Paige and Evan's story as much as I did writing it. Paige and Evan were both heartbroken from their marriages and they found it easier, each in their own way, to live without love. Better to be safe than to be hurt like that ever again. I wrote this story because I wanted to remind others that it's never too late for wonderful blessings to come into a person's life. True love can be just around the corner. As hard as it is to trust again, it is worth the risk to live with a whole and loving heart.

Wishing you peace and love,

Jillian Hart

## A FAMILY FOREVER

### BY

## BRENDA COULTER

When her fiancé was killed, pregnant Shelby Franklin's dreams were shattered. Tucker Sharpe was there to pick up the pieces and offer her a solution: marry him for the baby's sake. But would love for an unborn child be enough to keep them together?

**On sale March 2006**

*Available at your favorite retail outlet.*

**www.SteepleHill.com**

Steeple Hill®

LIAFFBC

# REQUEST YOUR FREE BOOKS!

## 2 FREE INSPIRATIONAL NOVELS
## PLUS A
## FREE
## MYSTERY GIFT

**YES!** Please send me 2 FREE Love Inspired® novels and my FREE mystery gift. After receiving them, if I don't wish to receive any more books, I can return the shipping statement marked "cancel." If I don't cancel, I will receive 4 brand-new novels every month and be billed just $3.99 per book in the U.S., or $4.74 per book in Canada, plus 25¢ shipping and handling per book and applicable taxes, if any*. That's a savings of over 20% off the cover price! I understand that accepting the 2 free books and gift places me under no obligation to buy anything. I can always return a shipment and cancel at any time. Even if I never buy another book from Steeple Hill, the two free books and gift are mine to keep forever.

113 IDN D74R  313 IDN D743

| | | |
|---|---|---|
| Name | (PLEASE PRINT) | |
| Address | | Apt. |
| City | State/Prov. | Zip/Postal Code |

Signature (if under 18, a parent or guardian must sign)

### Order online at www.LoveInspiredBooks.com

#### Or mail to Steeple Hill Reader Service™:

IN U.S.A.
3010 Walden Ave.
P.O. Box 1867
Buffalo, NY 14240-1867

IN CANADA
P.O. Box 609
Fort Erie, Ontario
L2A 5X3

Not valid to current Love Inspired subscribers.

**Want to try two free books from another series?**
**Call 1-800-873-8635 or visit www.morefreebooks.com**

* Terms and prices subject to change without notice. NY residents add applicable sales tax. Canadian residents will be charged applicable provincial taxes and GST. This offer is limited to one order per household. All orders subject to approval. Credit or debit balances in a customer's account(s) may be offset by any other outstanding balance owed by or to the customer.

LIREG05

# _Love Inspired_®

## TITLES AVAILABLE NEXT MONTH

### Don't miss these four stories in March

**WHEN DREAMS COME TRUE by Margaret Daley**
The Ladies of Sweetwater Lake

Zoey Witherspoon got the shock of her life when her estranged
husband showed up on her doorstep more than two years after
he was presumed dead in a plane crash. Though thrilled that he
was alive, Zoey struggled with giving her heart back to a man
who had the power to break it all over again.

**LESSONS FROM THE HEART by Dorothy Clark**

When newspaper reporter David Carlson and literacy worker
Erin Kelly teamed up for a story, there was an instant spark. But
when Erin discovered David's lack of faith, their budding romance
fizzled. David tried to move on, but when faced with adversity,
would he find himself drawn back to Erin and her God?

**A MATCH MADE IN BLISS by Diann Walker**
Part of the BLISS VILLAGE miniseries

Lauren Romey needed a vacation, so her friends suggested
a bed-and-breakfast. But when she wound up at the wrong
one, she found herself in the middle of a contest staged by
Garrett Cantrell's daughters—"Win Daddy's Heart." Lauren
wasn't looking for romance, but Garrett's love was an
appealing prize.

**A FAMILY FOREVER by Brenda Coulter**

When her fiancé was killed, pregnant Shelby Franklin feared she
wouldn't be able to provide for her unborn child. The marriage
of convenience proffered by the man who would have been her
brother-in-law was her only choice. Tucker Sharpe had promised
to look after Shelby, and he's determined to help her find love
again—with him.

LICNM0206